CW01506967

HOW TO COMMIT A
POSTCOLONIAL MURDER

HOW TO COMMIT A
POSTCOLONIAL MURDER

Nina McConigley

FLEET

FLEET

First published in the United States in 2026 by Pantheon Books,
A division of Penguin Random House LLC
First published in Great Britain in 2026 by Fleet

1 3 5 7 9 10 8 6 4 2

Copyright © 2026 by Nina McConigley

The moral right of the author has been asserted.

*All characters and events in this publication, other than those
clearly in the public domain, are fictitious and any resemblance
to real persons, living or dead, is purely coincidental.*

MASH game image © Abigail Gibbs
House blueprint image © Romano Nickerson

A CIP catalogue record for this book is available from the British Library.

Hardback ISBN 978-0-349-72535-2
Trade paperback ISBN 978-0-349-72536-9

Typeset in Janson
Composed by North Market Street Graphics,
Lancaster, Pennsylvania,
Designed by Casey Hampton
Printed and bound in Great Britain by Clays Ltd, Elcograf S.p.A

Papers used by Fleet are from well-managed forests
and other responsible sources.

Fleet
An imprint of
Little, Brown Book Group
Carmelite House
50 Victoria Embankment
London EC4Y 0DZ

The authorised representative
in the EEA is
Hachette Ireland
8 Castlecourt Centre,
Dublin 15, D15 XTP3, Ireland
(email: info@hbgi.ie)

An Hachette UK Company
www.hachette.co.uk

www.littlebrown.co.uk

For Lila—
my snow fence

The cook fed us meats of many kinds. I joined my belly to the belly of the next girl. It was pink and we opened our beaks for meat. It was wet and we licked the dictionary off each other's faces.

I've exhausted the alphabet. But I'm not writing this for you.

—Bhanu Kapil, *Humanimal*

They sped off, and Mr. Harris, after a reproachful glance, squatted down upon his hams. When English and Indians were both present, he grew self-conscious, because he did not know to whom he belonged. For a little he was vexed by opposite currents in his blood, then they blended, and he belonged to no one but himself.

—E. M. Forster, *A Passage to India*

CREEL FAMILY

Richard Creel
Indira Ayyar Creel
Agatha Krishna Creel
Georgette Ayyar Creel

AYYAR FAMILY

Vinod (Vinny) Ayyar
Devi Ayyar
Narayan (Ryan) Ayyar
Rajah (Thomas) Ayyar

MOORE FAMILY

Linda Moore
Ron Moore
Angel Moore
Bison Moore
Sonata Moore

CLAY FAMILY

Donald Clay
Mary Clay
Rosemary Clay
Beryl Clay

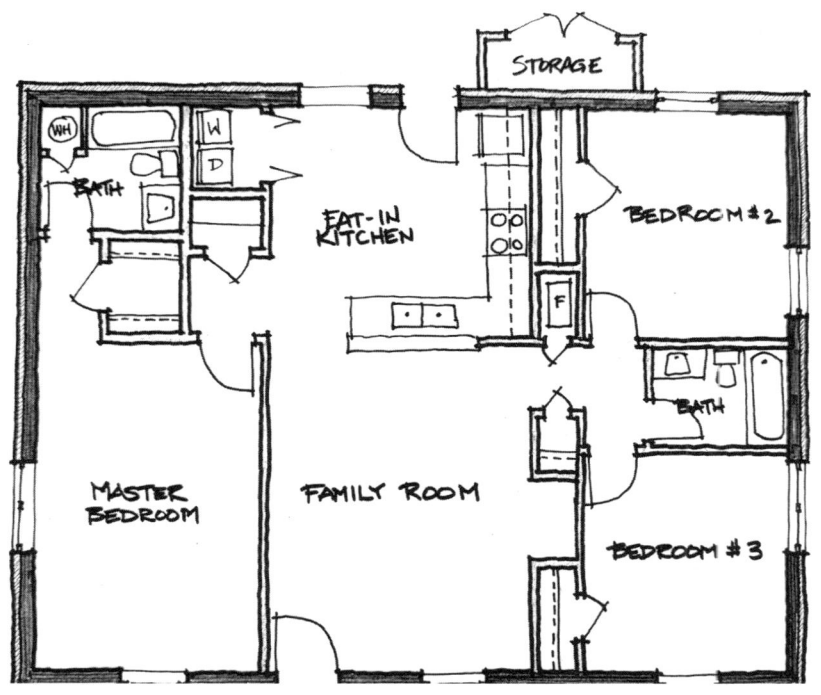

WH

BATH

EAT-IN KITCHEN

W

D

STORAGE

BEDROOM #2

F

BATH

MASTER BEDROOM

FAMILY ROOM

BEDROOM #3

THE CREEL HOME: COTTONWOOD CROSS

1986

HOW TO COMMIT A
POSTCOLONIAL MURDER

THE BLAME

My sister, Agatha Krishna, said it started when they came, and so that's where you could put the blame. But then she said we had to go further back than that. So we blamed it on Reagan; everyone blamed him that summer, the summer the country went into a bust, the summer we watched an exodus empty our town. Then I blamed the Cold War, and Gorbachev—he had the stain on his head, and thus, I felt, couldn't be trusted. We blamed famine in Ethiopia after Amma posted a photo on the fridge of a child with a belly like a hot-air balloon. We blamed AIDS, which we didn't really get, but thought you *could* get from the water fountain at the public library you stepped on with your foot. We blamed the Olympics and hated Sam the eagle, their feathered mascot, who dressed like Uncle Sam in red, white, and blue, though secretly I had a button of him with his sly smile and torch. We blamed it on my par-

ents for moving to Wyoming in the first place, for set-
tling in Marley. Then we just generally blamed them
for everything. We thought they shouldn't have married, that they shouldn't have mixed us up. Shouldn't
have made us halfies. Agatha Krishna said we could
blame it on our grandparents too, for having one child
who went to school and another who stayed at home.
For letting Amma wear a crisp, white uniform and leaving Vinny Uncle to read Curly Wee comics.

But then she said, "Let's blame it on the British."
Everything went back to the British. They did it first,
Agatha Krishna said. They were colonists. They were
the reason our amma went to school and our uncle
stayed home; they were the reason that we were quiet
around most white people, the reason our mom drank
tea when everyone else we knew, except Mormons,
drank coffee. It was the British who shaped Amma's
world. That made her spell *favor* with a *u*, use a knife
and fork, and bake fruitcake with sultanas and nuts. It
was the British who taught us to keep our upper lips
stiff at all times.

That year, we had an Indian summer twice. A frost
had come and left the garden in disarray. Tomato
stalks broke in two, my mother's peppers dangled like
limp green earrings from the stem. But then the days
warmed again and an infestation of millers descended.

They threw themselves in swarms at the streetlights, marking the intersections. They offered a kind of suttee to the light. Black dots against the Krishna-colored sky. My father, tired from coming off rigs, would fill a large stainless steel bowl with dish soap at night. Leaving it on his desk, he would shine a desk lamp into the soapy bowl. By morning, the bubbles would long have gone flat and the little bodies of the millers would be floating in the water, their wings soaked and black.

I always felt bad for them. Drawn to something beautiful, something almost ethereal, only to find themselves trapped. I didn't think it was a good way to die. But what is? And the only way you could justify it was when Amma held up saris eaten to lace, sweaters with holes the size of coins.

Years later, I would learn that miller moths don't eat clothes. They're actually great pollinators. We were wrong. Small clothes moths are the real pests. Clothes moths barely fly and don't like the light. But Appa didn't like the sound of the millers hitting the lights at night. Of them clogging the sills of our doors and windows with their downy scales.

It was in that second wave of warmth that they came to us. Not tired or wretched or tempest-tossed, but poor. We drove to Denver to pick them up. They did not come off the plane looking bewildered by this new land before them. If anything, they came at us like moths. Fast, a little frantic, and seemingly, as the months would show, drawn to all the wrong things.

Amma, who had not seen a member of her family since marrying my father almost fourteen years earlier, ran to her brother, Vinny Uncle, pressed a carton of Marlboro Reds into his pocket, then squeezed my cousin Narayan like a lemon and filled his hands with chocolate. She gave Auntie Devi a rhinestone necklace.

We piled into two cars to drive home. Narayan screamed when he saw his first antelope. Auntie Devi stuck her head out the window to catch the wind. Vinny Uncle just remarked on how fast the car went. That we didn't have to stop for animals in the road or pause at scooters packed with bodies.

The Ayyars dipped into our lives like a tea bag into the whiteness of a porcelain cup. They muddied the water and made our house feel small, having taken over Agatha Krishna's old bedroom. Now she slept with me. They left rings of talcum powder on the carpet; the bathroom floor was slick with water from their cup and bucket, and the house became smelly with the food Auntie Devi cooked: dosas and sambar, prawns fry and molee. If she wasn't cooking, she stood on the lawn in a sari and cardigan, looking out at nothing. Feeling the air and the altitude with a kind of wonder. Or sometimes she sat in front of the television. She watched a lot of *Dynasty*. She no longer had her own house; she didn't drive. She had to ask Amma to buy her everything, from underwear to airmail paper. To us, she said little, just cooked us food, then slipped back to the bedroom to watch TV late into the night. She was like Amma. Same long black hair. But not Amma. She was ghost-Amma. The Amma who didn't say anything. The Amma in the room who faded into the furniture. As if she had only half come to America.

When you really came down to it, we blamed our uncle. And no matter who started it, we were the ones who had to finish it. So at night, as we lay in bed, Agatha Krishna in a sleeping bag zipped tight to her head, and me under a blanket half-eaten by moths, we told ourselves that it wasn't our fault. She sang a mantra: "The British are to blame, the British are to blame, the British are to blame, and Vinny Uncle will pay." And soon, I joined her. We would make him pay.

Looking back, though, I'm not sure if that's how it works. I'm not sure you can ever cancel out someone who has taken from you by taking more from someone else. But I think that was the only way we could do it, the only way we could have killed him. The only way we could take our uncle's life and not look back. Not be filled with any blame.

1

YOU

But.

But before I give you that, before I tell you what happened, I have to give you this.

Because you ask for it, I give it to you.

Because you don't ask for it, I give it to you.

Because you always seem to want to take what I give you and translate it into something else, something that fits your narrative, you can have it.

Let's just say it. This story is for you; I know you want it to go a certain way.

I get it. We all do. And don't worry, I'll give you that story. But before we go back, before I tell you about the murder, about that year, I'll tell you this, just to get it out of the way. Here is what you want. Here it is as a list, so organized, so efficient:

1. Mangoes. I am going to give you mangoes. Fat, green globes of fruit. Green, because they are picked

too early and sent to Wyoming with only a hint of blush. These mangoes show up a few times a year. They are from Mexico, their taste a kind of thready sweetness, but my mother buys them anyway. We don't all like to eat mangoes. They're a heaty food, and my mother (*Amma, Amma, Amma*) makes us drink a large glass of milk an hour after we've had one to offset the heat she thinks will build in our stomachs. I hate milk. But when she serves us slices of mango with Tang, it's as if we're eating fire. She will chew on the seed for hours. Ripping off every piece of the flesh, the fibrous pit like a heart in her hand. She buries the seeds in pots, and we wait for a mango tree to bloom. It will not grow, even as Agatha Krishna and I grow other things—crystals for a science project, sprouts in a two-liter pop bottle that becomes a mini greenhouse—earning each of us a Girl Scout badge. But the mango never does. And yet somehow, there are always more mangoes. All the superstores have them. Now we can get them at Target, make eye contact with the other *others* as we reach for the fruit, as we squeeze the skin, as we wonder what the flesh is like, under that taut, green skin.

2. Saris. Only Aunt Devi wears saris. Sorry. Amma gave them up years ago. She wears jeans and sweat-

ers. When the Ayyars arrived, she wore saris again for a bit. But usually, they just sit on the top shelf of her closet, stacked one on top of another. Occasionally, one slides to the floor, the slipperiness of silk on silk, a pool of gold and incandescence on the carpet. Months after the Ayyars moved in, Amma and Aunt Devi went to JoAnn Fabrics to look through the bolts of fabric. I do not wear Indian clothes. Not because I don't want to, but because there is nowhere to buy a pavada, so I wear my own dresses to Indian functions. I don't like playing dress-up. I, who was soon to lose interest in Girl Scouts in favor of joining 4-H in the fall, would enter the fair with cotton Butterick dresses the following summer. I delighted in calico and sprigged lawn, neither of which hang well enough for a sari. I wanted to make a dove-in-the-window quilt like Laura Ingalls. But Amma and Aunt Devi bought six yards of various rayons. Unlike calico and sprigged lawn, rayon hangs well. They'd pull cholis out of their bags and match the spray of a tulip or the stem of a daisy to them. "Lots of fabric!" the lady at JoAnn would say. "Yes," said my mother. "There's so much to cover." It was true—sometimes we used Amma's saris to make a fort.

3. All the spices. All the food. You want this the most. And yet, there was nothing magical about our meals.

When my dad was on a rig, we often ate ramen, or bread with deviled ham. But sure, there was plenty of Indian food too. Dosas with ghee and sugar for breakfast, rasam when I had a cold, which Amma would make me drink from a small steel cup, one night's leftover rice turned to the next day's curd rice, dal that sat on the stove for days, never refrigerated, and curries. Lots of curries. We drove to Denver every so often to buy our spices. My job was to use the mortar and pestle to pound down garlic and ginger. My hands always smelled of somewhere else. When I went to Camp Sacajawea, which is now Camp Sacagawea, my mother tucked a jar with a tablespoon of curry powder inside my sleeping bag. She knew I would be homesick. Brushing my teeth by the small outdoor sinks, I'd dab some up my nose. To smell her, to smell home.

4. Wild animals. We did not have tigers. There were no elephants. But there was a small museum in town of one man's taxidermy collection. He'd shot a lot of African animals. Zebras, warthogs, antelopes with horns that looked like long, twisted lollipops. At one point he took to hunting in colder climes. A polar bear in an angry pose and an arctic fox graced a room that also held a walrus. This man, this rancher, shot everything, from elk to coyotes.

We knew that outside of town, and on the foothills of Marley Mountain, there were herds of antelope and deer. Occasionally there would be a rumor of a bear roaming around on the mountain. Campers would come out to find slashes in their duffels, pillowy bags of chips and coolers full of hot dogs gone. When Appa was home, he read us *The Jungle Book* at night, and we wondered which was more dangerous, a rattlesnake or Kaa.

5. Poverty. We weren't poor. We weren't rich. We were dependent on the price of oil. The Ayyars were beholden. But none of us was worse off than the boy on the fridge. The boy from Ethiopia, whose wide eyes and mound of a belly were the excuse Amma used to get us to eat anything she cooked for us. But you always ask: Aren't people poor in India? I guess. I don't know. I've never been. We did get free tuition at the Catholic school, all three of us: Agatha Krishna, me, and Narayan. To be fair, almost everyone did. Marley is an oil town, and we were in a *bust, bust, bust.*

6. Religion. We weren't Hindu; I know that's what you assumed. There are a lot of Christians in India. St. Thomas was martyred there. By the time we killed my uncle, we had been parishioners of

St. George's Episcopal Church for years, nearly all twelve years of my life. Agatha Krishna had just been confirmed the year before. For a while, our priest, Father Stewart, had been unsure if Agatha Krishna was ready to give a "mature public affirmation of her faith." His doubt stemmed from a worksheet she'd had to fill out on basic church vocabulary; when asked to explain what a bishop was, she answered: *a chess piece that can move diagonally*. But she was confirmed anyway. And because she, as an Episcopalian, had missed the pleasure of a first communion years ago when the rest of her class at school had received the Holy Sacrament, my mother allowed her to wear a white dress and veil for her confirmation. Most of the other kids wore starched Gunne Sax dresses and pressed khaki pants, but Agatha Krishna donned white from head to toe. She even wore a pair of white gloves I suspected she stole from the acolyte's closet in the church basement. I had seen her take a handful of Dubble Bubble from the Mini-Mart, forgetting the eighth commandment. But she gave me a few and knew I would not say a word.

7. Colonialism. There is some of that in this story. As I said, we blamed the British, whom we had no real sense of, as we knew no actual British people. But we blamed them whenever something went wrong. We

blamed them when it rained. We blamed them while we sipped milky tea instead of pop. We blamed them for Amma saying *to-mah-toe*. She, of course, liked the British, even if she never admitted it outright. She had gone to a British school, had followed the curriculum for the senior Cambridge exams in Madras, where she'd grown up. She could recite Shakespeare. She had once met Lady Baden-Powell, one of the founders of the Girl Guides, and her enthusiasm for Powell's mission is the reason that Agatha Krishna and I both were Girl Scouts. And then there were our names. I was named after Georgette Heyer—Georgie Ayyar Creel, a clever play on my mother's maiden name. Heyer was my mother's second-favorite writer. Her first was Agatha Christie, who, of course, was Agatha Krishna's namesake. She was always Agatha Krishna Akka to me, or AK Akka. Amma insisted I add the Akka. Though Agatha Krishna never called me Thangachi. Heyer and Christie wrote at more or less the same time. They were good wives and had both followed their husbands to places like the Caucasus Mountains and Tanganyika, Cairo and Baghdad. They both wrote mysteries, although Heyer was better known for her romances. My mother, as a schoolgirl in India, ate up Heyer's Regency stories just as she did Christie's tales of drawing rooms with Oriental rugs and cups of tea. Christie was later made a dame commander of the British Empire; Heyer never received any awards, but her husband was appointed Queen's Counsel. All of which is to say—we were named after proper white ladies, even if we ourselves were never proper anything.

8. Cows. Yes, there are a lot of cattle in Wyoming. Yes, I eat meat. Again, when Appa was away on rigs, Amma would serve us tins of meat. And hot dogs that floated in boiling water. Hamburger patties cooked until there was no pink left in them. At school we ate meat with names of people: sloppy joes, Salisbury steaks, and shepherd's pie. Amma did not consider chicken meat. Some nights she'd coat chicken in Shake 'n Bake, then grind pepper into the crumbs. She'd turn and turn the grinder until the chicken was almost gray.

9. Magical realism and/or the uncanny. Being of color is uncanny. Why do we need any more? You will always be exotic. Your skin a mystery. Your presence unsettling.

There—I think that's it. Now I can tell you the rest of the story without worrying that I've forgotten any of those details I know you're anticipating. Now I can be free to tell you the story I want to tell you, in exactly the way that I want to tell it. I'm not very good at this ventriloquist act. I am, after all, half-and-half. People tend to be fascinated by half-and-half beings. The fat Ganesha with his elephant head and pudgy man body. The jackalope with horns like a gate behind its ears. Mermaids, centaurs, satyrs, and sphinxes. All peculiar. Me, I take my skin—which is brown, not blue—and gather you round like Gopis.

Does it bother me that you want to hear the story this way? Yes. Does it make me angry that you need all of these specific details to feel like you're reading a proper brown-person story? Yes.

But what did I ever do to you? you say. *I'm not the one who made the world this way,* you say.

And then you're blaming the colonists too—but, of course, you're nothing like them.

Aren't I allowed to be angry though? Even just sometimes? Usually, I work hard to please, keep my head down. But now, let me be angry.

And if you're lost, if you have no idea what I'm talking about . . . If you're wondering what the big deal is . . . It's brownness. It's being the Other. It's having to perform. It's what happens when people are split, when countries are split. I have been performing forever. My own little dance. But I'm going to stop now. You can take it. I've been taking it my whole life.

2

JANUARY

Everything fell apart that year.

It started with the *Challenger*.

When things split in two, they aren't always half-and-half. Look at India. The top of it got completely cut off. The British offed its head in one fell swoop, and suddenly there wasn't just India, there was Pakistan too.

Or take Marley. Marley started as Fort Marley, which was a US base on Arapaho land. Then *chop, chop, chop*—the Arapaho were sent to a reservation, and the fort became a town. And the government didn't give them even a whole head; they just got a finger of land. Lieutenant Amos Marley gave his head, though, when the Arapaho attacked Fort Marley later. He was scalped.

We visited Fort Marley every year. Half our class would go dressed as Indians, the other half as cowboys. Most of the kids wanted to be cowboys. We were always Indians. My mother would weave a peacock feather from a vase on her dresser into my braids. She'd fashion a vest out of a paper grocery bag, and for a skirt, I wore a brown sari petticoat cut in half and then cut again to make a fringe. Once we got there, we'd reenact the Battle of Fort Marley. Heather Ross, a girl who'd sneered at my coconut-oil-greased hair since first grade, dressed as a cowboy. She would come at me. She'd ask me to take her (clean, dry) hair, hand me a stick, and say, "Scalp me!" But I didn't have it in me to kill then, so I'd go outside and wait with Narayan. We'd sit on wagon wheels while our classmates pretended to kill one another.

There were so many divisions that year. Our house, Cottonwood Cross, split in two. Amma and Aunt Devi each taking to their rooms. Auntie Devi, who had long ago accepted her arranged marriage, had at least had the upper hand in India. She had no mother-in-law there and was used to being in charge. Vinny Uncle had asked for a Vijai Super Deluxe scooter for his dowry. Auntie Devi made him sell it within a year. But now there was Amma, who, as Vinny Uncle's akka, was used to telling him what to do. They both circled him, tightening their imaginary reins. Each one of them asking him to pick up groceries (milk for Auntie Devi, bread for Amma), take out the trash, watch us. If Auntie Devi wasn't cooking or watching TV, she was usually sulking. We could hear her and Vinny Uncle arguing through the door. AK Akka listened with a cup to the door. She said Auntie Devi missed home. She hated Agatha Krishna's room. She thought Amma kept the house too cold, and she wanted her own *TV Guide* so that she could circle the shows she wanted to watch.

Agatha Krishna got her period and *split, split, split* from being a girl. She wore oversize sweatshirts and hid her chest with a cardigan over her uniform. But she and I had split before that. We had been split for months. Vinny Uncle had made sure of that.

The *Challenger* split into so many parts you couldn't tell what was what. We watched it in our classroom, our teacher Mrs. Lynch scrambling to roll the TV out of the room on its little cart when she realized what was happening. It was the first tragedy I had seen on TV. It was years before it would become the norm to watch horrors unfold in real time.

After it happened, we put down the apple flags we'd been waving in support of the first teacher in space. We spent the rest of the afternoon playing "heads-up, seven-up" while Mrs. Lynch cried at her desk.

What does NASA stand for?

Need Another Seven Astronauts.

A dumb joke that Heather Ross spit out on the playground. My stomach sank, hearing it. What did she know about being blown apart?

AK Akka and I, we split when we were born. As soon as we were out of Amma. Half brown, half white. We split at school too, the only brown kids. We were ink spots in class photos. In high school, my nickname was Mino because I was one of the few minorities in the school. We split, were other, and that was that.

And then Vinny Uncle came and split us right through our middles. Before him, we may have been others at school, but at home, we were linked like two chains. Appa would have to come into our rooms several times throughout the night to get us to stop jumping on the beds, reading our *'Teen* magazine out loud to each other, or feasting on snacks we'd smuggled in from the kitchen. We were never apart. But then Vinny Uncle came, and he started in on AK Akka first, and me later. He'd take one of us into the bathroom with him, and when we came back out, we'd be split, from each other, from ourselves.

After he was done, there was the me who was *me* and the me who was *you*, a part of myself that was separate, split outside of my body.

It's like that poem—do you know it?

I have a little shadow that goes in and out with me,
And what can be the use of him is more than I can see.
He is very, very like me from the heels up to the head;
And I see him jump before me, when I jump into my bed.

*The funniest thing about him is the way he likes to
  grow—
Not at all like proper children, which is always very
  slow;
For he sometimes shoots up taller like an india-rubber
  ball,
And he sometimes gets so little that there's none of him
  at all . . .*

Vinny Uncle made us shadow people. He made us
see outside ourselves. And what we saw was dark,
unformed. It was a not-sure-if-we-were-bad-or-good
feeling. Not-sure-it-was-wrong-or-right feeling. It was
a not-sure-if-we-were-girls-or-women feeling. Not-
sure-of-secrets feeling. Not-sure-what-is-a-secret feeling. He said not to tell anyone or he would have to
go back to India and Amma would be sad. So a not-
ever-talked-about feeling. Sometimes it felt small, easy
to hide away; sometimes it felt big, so big we couldn't
see anything beyond it. Because what I see now is that
being a person is like being an india-rubber ball—
neither should ever be split down the middle. I had to
take back my shadow, keep it tightly within me.

And while what we did changed our family in ways
I would never be able to change back, I never was sorry
he was gone. After he was gone, I only ever saw my
shadow in the sun.

. . .

The *Challenger* exploded at the end of January—always a bad month in Marley. The snow holds the pulp of winter: lost mittens, dog shit, forgotten hoses, unraked leaves all matted together. The wind clots trash along the fences. Plastic bags, scraps of paper, empty cans. There are bluebird skies but bitter cold. The roads are packed ice. I-25 closes again and again as semis skid off the highway. The snow melts and freezes. And you live with the knowledge that it will be like that for months longer.

We didn't celebrate anything in January then. No Martin Luther King Jr. Day. No Lunar New Year. Our town didn't start to celebrate those days until later, when other people—white people—decided to support the other, at least for show. When ordering bao and posting quotes on social media about light driving out darkness let you feel like you were doing "the work." There was none of that then, no break from the relentless cold.

We left our tree up until Epiphany that year, as we often did. The needles had pooled on the floor by January. The angels hung on to bare branches. It was the Ayyars' second Christmas with us; the novelty was gone. Narayan already knew that the man at the Prairie Mall wasn't really Father Christmas. He already knew that he and I would be asked to play Mary and Joseph in the school Christmas pageant because Jesus was a Jew from the Middle East and we were the only brown people in our class. Everyone thought we should be honored to get those roles, so we played husband and wife. Again.

The Ayyars may have stayed, but really, Marley was a town made for passing through. We were firmly founded in 1888 AD (though the Arapaho would tell you otherwise). Amma had told us that in two years the town would celebrate its centennial. I don't think that impressed the Ayyars. India was older than Jesus and Mary. Marley was just where people crossed the North Platte River on their way farther west. Our founders were the people who had gotten tired on the trail, who'd gotten out of their wagons and said enough was enough. Evidence: four major trails passed through the town—the Oregon Trail, the California Trail, the Mormon Trail, and the Pony Express route. And now there's the interstate. The highway. This wasn't the part of Wyoming where people lingered. It's not the pretty Wyoming, the tourist Wyoming. It's the real one.

Because I'm sure you've heard: Wyoming is beautiful. The Tetons—perfection. Yellowstone—America at its finest. Jackson Hole—*cute, cute, cute!* You like to ski? Great. You want to see a bison? We got 'em! And don't forget Devils Tower; it rises out of the prairie like a great lingam.

But Marley. Firmly oil and gas land. Refineries greet you on either end of town. Marley Mountain rises out of the south like a fold of fat on the prairie. The mountain is a fault scarp, a broken face of rock where the Precambrian fabric ripped and buckled upward, parting from the lower plate on which the town now sprawls, exposing the deep Paleozoic sandstones and limestones and laying bare the ancient igneous basement. A sparse mix of bitterbrush and sage surrounds the town, springing from the thin soil derived from the underlying Cretaceous shale. Beneath the surface lie the preserved fossils of sea creatures and dinosaurs waiting to be dug up. How do I know this? I'm a geologist's daughter. Appa spent car trips pointing out slumps and saddles and shale.

Appa's job was earth, and in Marley, the earth was there for extraction. You can pull almost anything out of the earth. Trees, vegetables, fish, diamonds, oil, gas, people. All these things are seemingly just there for the taking. When I asked him if it was okay to take oil, if the land would be okay after, he always said yes. We needed to drive our cars, he said. And anyway, the places his rigs were weren't beautiful. It was okay to take what you needed.

Appa was always working on wells. His job was taking oil from the earth. That's how he made money, but that year, there was no money. He mud-logged and did any jobs he could.

Appa always brought me something back when he came home from the rigs. He found things on the prairie: beads from tribes long gone, a small antler shed, bits of bone and vertebrae from antelope. He'd come home from the man camps in a daze. Home to a house full of Indians. He'd set down his sleeping bag and equipment and make himself a cup of coffee. He was the only one who drank it. After spending weeks checking depths and operations, he often went to bed for days. But no matter how much he slept, when he was home, we were safe. Vinny Uncle never bothered us then.

Appa would read to us at night. Usually folktales from his childhood, though once he told me and Agatha Krishna that he'd give us both ten dollars if we could memorize the geologic time chart. *Cretaceous. Jurassic. Triassic. Permian. Carboniferous. Devonian. Silurian. Ordovician. Cambrian.*

And he'd tell us how to get oil from the earth, gas from the rocks.

There were many steps to extraction.

1. Exploration: Geologists look at maps and seismic surveys and studies to identify oil reservoirs.

2. Drilling the well: A hole is drilled into the earth's crust, through many different rock layers, until you hit the reservoir.

3. Casing the well: A steel casing is inserted into the drilled hole to prevent it from collapsing. Cement is pumped into the casing to secure it in place and to isolate the different rock layers.

4. Completion and production: Production tubing and other equipment are added to the well to make sure completion happens—that oil can now flow into the wellbore. You must perforate the tubing. You don't want the tube to close in on itself.

5. Extraction and surface facilities: The oil comes to the surface through the wellhead. Facilities like separators and storage tanks are used to separate out the oil, gas, and water until it's ready to use.

That was the bread and butter of the Wyoming we grew up in, and that work of extraction left its mark on the land. Still, there were some places on Marley Mountain that were pleasant. Places where, in the autumn, when the aspens turned, you could take a picnic and feel like you were somewhere beautiful. But mostly it was covered in lodgepole pines that were blighted by pine beetle—just one big ghost forest.

There's the reservoir west of town, though, surrounded by red rock canyons. You can fish—get a boat, hook trout, kokanee salmon, walleye.

Marley has some other attractions too. It has, for instance, the largest mall in Wyoming. Prairie Mall. *Discover it all at Prairie Mall,* they say.

There are four big stores, among them JCPenney. The first JCPenney was in Kemmerer, Wyoming, which is almost four and a half hours away from Marley. James Cash Penney was the son of a Baptist preacher, and his father made him start paying for his own clothes when he was eight. He was born in Missouri but moved west when he caught tuberculosis. Don't you know that mountain air heals everything? He worked hard for a store called the Golden Rule, and the owners were impressed by his work ethic. They gave him a small partnership in a new store, which he called the J. C. Penney Stores Company. In 1940, he taught a young man named Sam Walton how to wrap packages in his store in Iowa. Sam Walton later founded Walmart.

There are two Walmarts in Marley now, but in 1986, there were none. There was a Kmart and a Buttrey's, from which Agatha Krishna once stole a blue eye shadow. They were both near the highway. Everything in Marley was. The stretch of highway near our house, Cottonwood Cross, had been adopted by the Daughters of the American Revolution, and twice a year their gray heads nodded like pump jacks along the roadway, picking up the litter of car trips and the debris of the Wyoming wind. Amma and Appa never thought Marley would be where they would stop. But once there was nothing left to extract, there wasn't anywhere else to go.

Cottonwood Cross. Our house originally had no name. It was my mother who named it, who began its recorded history, though it had had two owners before us. One was another oil worker, the other an insurance agent. My sister and I found a box of notepads that had the insurance agent's logo emblazoned on them; we used them for years, never knowing Eugene Johnson or exactly how he could meet your insurance needs.

Usually it's the rich who name their houses. Manors, halls, houses, castles, and lodges. Even cottages. Street numbering began in Britain in 1765, following an Act of Parliament. Odd numbers are usually on the left side of the street, and even numbers are on the right. To name your house before numbers was practical. It stated a surname, a location, what the building's original use was—an abbey or gatehouse, perhaps. It showed history, longevity. Something our family did not have in Wyoming. We lived in Marley for work. So that Appa could extract oil and gas out of the ground. But Amma didn't like simply living at 2216 Kit Carson Drive. She wanted to write home to her father in India with tales of something grander. She knew nothing about the frontier, really. For her, the great frontier was Cottonwood Cross itself, her own little homestead.

Cottonwood Cross was an even. Right on the curve of a cul-de-sac. We were not a lodge or a cottage. We were a ranch. A ranch house within an actual ranch. Our house was built on the old CY Ranch's land. You knew someone was an outsider if they pronounced CY like *sigh* instead of *see, why*. But all that was left of the ranch when I lived there was the name it had given to the main road through town. A former stock trail that led to the railroad. But it reminded us all that this was once a real ranch. The rich name things after themselves, after their history. But we were not rich, and our house wasn't an old vicarage, or a mill house, or a rectory, or a grange. We could not be the old anything. All the houses in our neighborhood were built for an oil boom. They were all 1950s flat-roofed, single-storied sprawls. They were all new. This whole country was new.

At first, Amma had wanted to name the place after an animal. Squirrel's Leap. Deer's Rest. Robin's Nest. Then she proposed Lilac Cottage. There was a row of lilac bushes alongside the house that never bloomed;

the frost killed them every year around Mother's Day—we got a single sprig of closed lilac one year to put on Amma's breakfast-in-bed tray. That was it.

She suggested Creekside Cottage next—there was a creek behind the house. But ultimately, above all, the property was defined by its cottonwoods; that was why my parents had fallen for it. My mother, who missed the greenery of India, had wanted trees. She hadn't been able to resist the large cottonwood that fanned over our roof in the front of the house, or the three others that bordered the yard in the back. She told us about trees in Madras: flame of the forest trees, frangipani, rain trees, neem trees. Later she would plant spruce trees in the backyard, attempting to have something green all winter long. The ring of cottonwoods around the house felt claustrophobic to me, but to Amma, it was a nice change from how *open, open, open* Wyoming always seemed to be.

As I said, Cottonwood Cross was on Kit Carson Drive. Kit Carson was a frontiersman. A trapper. He killed Indians. The next street over was Jim Bridger. The street after that was William Cody Avenue. Then Custer Street. Then Fetterman. Then Fremont. What a lot of explorers. We may not name houses in Wyoming, but we name streets after men. Men who took one look at the Arapaho, Shoshone, Cheyenne, and Sioux living here and decided to further their westward expansion. They extracted the land from the Indians long before we started extracting the oil from the land.

The biggest cottonwood tree on Kit Carson Drive, the biggest cottonwood we'd ever seen, was in the Bensons' yard, at the top of the cul-de-sac. Angel Moore, who did not live on our street but seemed always to be at her aunt's house next door to us, told us that years ago, when this was still the CY Ranch, the ranchers hanged Indians from that tree. I'm not sure, ultimately, if I found the tree scary because of its stature or because it was haunted.

Not long before we killed my uncle, we started playing hangings on that tree. Over the course of that summer, we hanged my cousin and most of the Mitchell children off a low branch with a clothesline. The Bensons were at work and never knew what we did in their yard every day. Agatha Krishna was always the one to kick the stool out from under whomever's turn it was to die. I think she wanted the practice. To see if we had the grit to kill. Already I balked. I hung back while she and Angel paraded whoever's turn it was to our noose. I knew the acrylic yarn Angel took from her aunts wouldn't kill anyone. But I also knew *thou shalt not kill.* I didn't want to kill anyone. And yet we played God anyway. We recorded their crimes, from stealing to dog rustling, on a Eugene Johnson notepad, and then they hanged for them.

Years later I would see, recorded on that same notepad in Agatha Krishna's clear cursive: *Vinod Ayyar: sinner.*

The plains cottonwood has been the state tree of Wyoming since 1947. A potent year all around—the year of India's independence, the year the country split in two.

Let's go back. In the months leading up to India's independence, my grandmother became nervous. Her family was neither Hindu nor Muslim, and she wasn't sure how they'd all fit into this new India. They lived in Madras, on Barnaby Road, far away from Lahore and the new line that scalped the country, jutting like a snout into what would soon become Pakistan. When rioting started across the partition line up north, only small waves were felt in Madras. Trifling disputes broke out in sputters in markets and in front of train stations. But it was enough for Hindus and Muslims to look at each other with a slow side-eye, with suspicion. My grandmother, my paati, whom I would never meet, was vexed. She was ever practical, and so bought cheap wooden rosaries made out of the seeds of lotuses—or was it aloe? My mother could never remember what they were made of. But Vinny Uncle was sly even then. He chewed on the rosary as a snack and told my mother if she planted the beads, a tree would grow. His tall tales aside, though, my grandmother put those rosaries around her children's necks every morning in the days leading up to August 15, and well after, and trained them to be as nonpartisan as possible when it came to the partition.

"Tell anyone who asks that you're Christian. This line has nothing to do with us!" she warned. "If anyone says anything to you, just start saying the Our Father," she advised. "This split has nothing to do with us!"

And thus began weeks of beggars and shopkeepers alike being given bits of prayers from my amma and Vinny Uncle, rather than responses to the questions they'd asked of them.

"One paisa?" asked an unsuspecting beggar, only to be met with a fervent "Hallowed be thy name!"

When the candy man gave my mother a long look after she'd ordered tutti frutti, she exclaimed, "Give us this day our daily bread!" And so he brought her a spongy piece of white bread. Clean and flat with her shake.

It was a tactic that Agatha Krishna and I tried to use ourselves when we didn't want to answer a question. We'd say the Hail Mary instead. If a teacher, or even my mother, asked why we were sullen, why we hadn't done something we were meant to do: "Blessed be the fruit of thy womb, Jesus."

My mother went to a school called Doveton Corrie, named after Captain John Doveton. He was mixed, just like us. An Anglo-Indian who played a role in some British campaigns in Afghanistan and India and later bequeathed in his will fifty thousand pounds for the purpose of education. And even though he died in England, that money led to the formation of a school and a college in Calcutta. Later, a school in Madras. Vinny Uncle didn't go there, but he went briefly to Don Bosco, a school named after an Italian priest who later became a saint. He never showed any aptitude for education; he spent most of his time wandering the streets of Kilpauk, playing cards and roughhousing with older boys.

On August 15, 1947, all the girls at Doveton gathered around the flagpole. My mother tucked her rosary into her starched white uniform as they sang "God Save the King" one last time before the Union Jack came down. The new Indian flag—orange, white, and green, with the blue Ashoka wheel—went up. They worked their way through the new national anthem, the "Jana Gana Mana," but since most of them were Tamil or Anglo-Indian, they struggled with the lyrics. *Jaya he, jaya he, jaya he, Jaya jaya jaya, jaya he!* The Bengali and Sanskrit words turned in their Tamil mouths like rosary beads, bitter and unpalatable.

That afternoon when Amma and Vinny Uncle came home from school, they found their grandfather Rajah Thomas Ayyar, who called himself Thomas, and not

Rajah, sitting at the kitchen table, two books in front of him.

My great-grandfather was a former inspector at a match factory and now lived in Kerala. He had traveled up that day for what he felt was not just the beginning of India but the beginning of a new chapter for the Ayyars. We were free from the British now, and he believed that we needed a new language to mark the occasion.

"India began its life as a nation today," he told them in English, though switched to Tamil to address my grandmother. "We are now unified as a modern country and need a modern language to bring us together—what do you suppose that should be?"

My uncle, perhaps expecting a trick, replied: "Hindi?"

"No."

They knew it couldn't have been Tamil.

"English?" my mother guessed.

"No."

"Sanskrit!" Vinny Uncle shouted, adding a *jaya he* to suck up.

"No!" Thomas reached for the books and opened the first one. *BASIC ESPERANTO* was typed in bold letters on the first page.

"*Saluton!*" he exclaimed. "Your mother and father, you, and your brother are going to learn the language of the future. Look at India! All muddled. Do we speak

Hindi? Do we speak Tamil? Do we speak English? I say we need a language that unites us all. A Utopian language! From here on, we will all speak the language that the whole world will be speaking one hundred years from now. *Kiel vi sanas?*" he asked the mute faces of his family.

Thatha's pen friend in England had told him about Esperanto. He was an immediate convert. No one could misunderstand each other if we all had a common language that favored no one! Thatha had gone to the Bengali Institute of Esperanto to learn and spent every morning after his bath taking tea and studying.

For years, Thomas Thatha spoke only Esperanto, to the silence of his children and grandchildren. Eventually he gave up, but he held firmly to his belief that the British (whose fruitcake and cologne he delighted in) used language to gain supremacy. Renaming all the streets and cities in India. He would tell his children and grandchildren all the words that were actually Indian: *punch, bungalow, juggernaut, jodhpurs, loot.* He wouldn't be alive when the names all switched back again, when Madras became Chennai.

"We need to make our own language, Georgie. Like Thatha," Agatha Krishna decided. "I already have a few words. *Yuckaduck* is when something is really bad. *Keeliti* is when something is really good. And *yoodleup* is a really stupid person."

"Yoodleup," I repeated, laughing.

She pinched my arm. "We need our own language. This is something new. We are our own country."

"Ow." I rubbed my arm.

"This needs to be for only us," she said. "We need something new. For only us."

There was no talking to Agatha Krishna when she pinched me.

Yuckaduck. Yuckaduck. That month was so much yuckaduck.

We never got beyond those three words. But strangely they served us well for many years. A quick *yuckaduck* or *yoodleup* said more between us than anything else. It was our own constructed language, something only we could understand. We already knew each other's looks and expressions. I could read AK Akka even when she was coated in Noxzema.

Our great-grandfather had language far beyond our small vocabulary. He would have full conversations with other Esperanto devotees in coffee shops. Other lonely men like him. He had pen pals too, in places as far away as Poland and France, to whom he wrote long letters in their shared language. The name *Esperanto* means "one who hopes," and that summed up Thomas very well indeed. *Unu lingvo neniam estas sufiĉa,* he wrote—"One language is never enough." *Mi feliĉasm*—"I'm happy." *Ĝis la revido!*—"See you later!"

Poor great-grandfather Thomas. Esperanto never caught on, though there are still clubs all over India that speak it. But Thatha's dream of uniting India with Esperanto never came to fruition. His dream of one spoken language for the world's largest democracy was a bust. Though, really, language was the least of the concerns of the new Indian nation.

Thatha's main pen friend was a Mr. Clay, to whom he wrote for years. Mr. Clay lived in England, in the Lake District, and drove a red Rover. Pen friends were big in our family. I had one too, years later; she lived in Kenya and her name was Joy Ouma. I told her all my secrets. Even that we'd killed a man. To which she wrote back, "Americans! You're so funny." I stopped writing soon after that.

I wonder if there was a moment when the British knew the jig was up. That they had to leave. Were they watching one of Gandhi's speeches? Was it just a matter of money (or lack thereof) after the war? They were sunk. They had divided and divided the world, and now had pieces so small, they were slipping through their fingers.

Vinny Uncle never knew the jig was up. That it was time for him to go. To *split, split, split* away from us. But we knew. We knew when we heard his door open at night. We knew when my mother left for the grocery store. We knew when the bathroom door was closed. We knew when we smelled his cigarette smoke. When we heard the TV turn up loud.

To have freedom, there is always a fight. Sometimes you lose part of yourself. Sometimes you gain something altogether different from what you thought. And sometimes which side is right and which side is wrong gets all muddled together.

It was an unseasonably warm day that January when we found our neighbors' cat, Tom Cat Pops, dead under a tree in the backyard. A black mark in the snow. We picked him up, his stiff body flat and inflexible. Poor Pops. He was a terrible cat. He often jumped into our bedroom window at night; the screen had been ripped to holes for years. Pops didn't let you cuddle him. He hissed and wriggled out of your arms. He wasn't made for loving. And now there he was, dead under a cottonwood, with no sign at all as to what had killed him.

"That cat, the Mitchells' cat. It ate antifreeze," we heard our father tell Amma a week or two later. "Annie Mitchell thinks someone killed it on purpose. Which is rich."

I didn't think it was so rich. No one liked that cat.

But Amma was quiet. She was putting it together. She had killed the cat.

A few weeks earlier, there had been antifreeze pooled in our driveway. The snow had covered it for a bit, but then it came back. My father had been on a rig, and my mother only bothered to clean it up when she found me and Agatha Krishna dipping our Barbies' toes into the iridescent green puddle of ooze. Vinny Uncle had taken Amma's car to buy cigarettes. Agatha Krishna didn't like to admit she still liked Barbies. But she was always making up dramatic plays for them: She cut off Golden Dream Barbie's hair so she could be Cancer Barbie, or right that moment, our Barbies were trying to survive a nuclear disaster. We lived 180 miles from the missile base in Cheyenne and had secretly watched a made-for-TV movie about nuclear war. I was terrified of turning to ash, evaporating away.

"Get a bucket of water," Amma told Agatha Krishna.

"Use this brush," she said to me.

We cleaned the driveway, and when we were done, she moved the car back over the stained spot.

That night, she tucked us in and paused outside the door.

"Please don't tell your father the car was leaking." She'd taken it in on the sly to a mechanic. She was sure she would be blamed for any car problem that arose on her watch. That was why we'd never told my father about the time Amma had gotten a ticket and pretended not to understand English as the red-faced American cop spoke loud and slow: "Now, in our country, you have to STOP when you see those signs. Not slow down." Or the time she'd stopped in the parking lot of the Gibson's while looking for her keys and let go of her cart. She just stood and watched as it careened slowly into a parked Pinto, then hastily told me to go get it. She knew Appa would be mad. That our insurance would go up. So we got in the car and left. We didn't leave a note.

"Antifreeze is sweet. Pops didn't even know what he was eating. He must have thought it was a treat." She had called the mechanic that afternoon, was repeating to us what he had told her.

"We won't say a word," said Agatha Krishna.

Later I saw her in the garage. Sniffing the bottle and trying a little bit on the tip of her finger.

It was after my mother turned out the light that Agatha Krishna pushed her bed next to mine. She curled into me. Her body in the crack between the mattresses. She scratched my back.

"I know how we're going to be free," she said. "I know exactly what we need to do."

Shadows marked the wall of our room. I wasn't sure what she meant. I wasn't sure if she meant we should tell Appa or something else. It didn't matter anyway. There was only one word that seemed right to say.

"Keeliti," I said. I'd had only three options.

3

YOU

So I mentioned the Indians. You love Indians. Both kinds. You cannot be from these United States and say something bad about Indians. And you know what, you shouldn't. They were here before Ellis Island, before the *Mayflower*.

You love *Dances with Wolves*. You like to gamble at reservation casinos—but oh, they also make you so sad. You have a Navajo rug in your house. You *had* a spirit animal—no more, of course, but it was your dog, so sweet and loyal. You like your Native jewelry. A turquoise ring. A cuff with patterns and an inlay of mother-of-pearl and coral. A silver thunderbird neck-lace. You like that you can look down at that little sea in a stone on your hand and be reminded of the time you posed in front of antler arches. The time you saw the Grand Canyon. A shoot-out in Tombstone. Drove on Route 66. A modern memento mori to remind you of death. That is, to show you were alive. You saw the orange of the canyons, the blue of the Tetons, the brown of the desert.

It's not your culture. But it's not dressing up. It's not like Pocahontas or Tiger Lily. You would never.

But also—you're confused. *Can you help me?* you ask. *Is it* Indigenous? Native? American Indian? Native American? *Or should you say the tribe's name? But there are so many names.*

Why does everyone demand to be known?

But this story isn't even about that, you say. *You're the other kind of Indian.*

But you don't see. How you dip and take and appreciate us both. How your appreciation becomes appropriation.

If you take India: Eat the food. Watch Bollywood. Laugh at the comedians on TV. There are so many of them now. Do the yoga. Namaste. Celebrate Diwali with a little lamp. Oil your hair. Vote for Kamala. Tell me that there are others who are so much worse off. Tell me that your doctor is Indian. That so many Catholic priests are from India now. That you can't understand them when they say the Lord's Prayer! Ha ha ha!

I am tired of it all. I live with you, among white people. I lived with my appa. And so perhaps I am being unfair. Microaggressions—even the word makes me tired. But here's the thing: I call it something else. You want me to perform culture in a certain way. To tell you a story a certain way. To tell you about stinky lunches and how hard it was to be us. When I think it must be hard to be you. Your culture so vague.

Of course, later in high school, my Indianness had currency—I made up yoga moves and waxed on about vegetarianism, just for a laugh.

I was in ninth grade when I had to take a course called Hunter Safety. It's what we did instead of gym class. We went to a rifle range and practiced shooting with pellet guns. I was a good shot, I learned. Afterward, we cleared the range, picking up the discarded pellets. Later, Sharon Clapp, a ranch kid who would miss weeks of school in the spring during lambing, brought in a stillborn lamb to teach us how to field dress an animal. We gathered around and took out its organs, skinned it, drained it. I held its heart in my hand.

Hunter-gatherers. The two ways of being. That was what our textbooks said.

We had always been gatherers. Amma said to us that Gandhi told Indians not to cooperate. Not to pick tea. Not to pick cotton. No more gathering.

But I had no time for that now. Simply to stop gathering wasn't enough. We had tried months of non-violence. We were done gathering. I was ready to hunt.

4

FEBRUARY

Every year around February 3, a priest would come to our class and bless our throats. He took two unlit candles and crossed them, put them up to our necks, and said a blessing to St. Blaise, an intercession that our throats would stay pink, that no illness would come to pass. St. Blaise had once cured a boy who had a fish bone lodged in his throat. The boy was choking; he could not breathe. His mother had pleaded for his life, and St. Blaise cured him. The bone flew out of his mouth. The boy could speak again. The boy could eat again.

Is it a blessing to be able to speak? Is it a blessing to tell the truth?

Once, after the blessing, I got lice. My head crawled with them. My mother pulled out a small wooden comb she'd brought from Madras. She rubbed coconut oil into my hair and *combed, combed, combed.* After a while, she grew tired. She took out her sewing shears and *cut, cut, cut.* I watched my hair fall to the ground, like black fish on the floor, like black mollies, X's on the tic-tac-toe of the kitchen tile, scalped right there in the kitchen.

There would be no Barbizon audition for me. Or for Agatha Krishna, who, two days later, had her own haircut. She had a copy of the Barbizon handbook and told me she was in training. There was a catwalk set up at the Prairie Mall for a full fashion show that very weekend. Agatha Krishna, AK Akka, was to wear a sweatshirt with puppies and the phrase *PUP SQUAD* on it. Every night that winter, she ran the water in the bathroom sink as hot as it would go. Then dipped a hot washcloth under the stream. She'd wring it out and put it on her face. She was opening her pores. Then she would spread a thick layer of Noxzema all over her face. That white face. She would sit and read magazines while she waited for her pores to heal. *YM* told us to *steam, steam, steam. Seventeen* told us to *rinse, rinse, rinse.* After she cleaned off the cream, she'd *dab, dab, dab* with Sea Breeze for perfect skin.

I dared not use any of her products, which she laid out carefully on our dresser. Five of us shared the bathroom, and AK Akka didn't want Narayan or Auntie Devi to use her soaps and lotions. She babysat and weeded for a neighbor in order to buy them. Sometimes I'd take a small scoop of Noxzema and rub it into my cheeks, inhaling the coolness. I didn't have any acne, but Agatha Krishna had a sprinkle. On weekends, she'd empty a chamomile tea bag into a bowl of boiling water and put a white towel over her head as she absorbed the steam. She looked like a ghost. Often she'd make a bowl for me too, and set the kitchen timer. After five minutes we'd both take the towels off and laugh at our sweaty faces, gulp at the cool air. It was the one beauty ritual we did together. I passed when she started making egg-yolk masks. She looked jaundiced, or like Auntie Devi did when she spread a turmeric mask on her face. I had no interest in things like that then. The only thing I valued was a small soap shaped like a rose, which I kept on the dresser as well. I never used it. Eventually I realized that somehow it had gotten lost.

Auntie Devi and Amma didn't get lice from us, so they kept their long hair. They oiled it regularly, so all the pillowcases in our house had little translucent spots on them that would never wash out. Other women were always trying to touch their hair. At JCPenney. At church. At Gibson's. They couldn't resist running a hand down their backs, touching their shiny black flags.

I liked having my hair short. No one touches you when you're ugly.

Our now-neighbor Angel Moore told us we were like Samson. She looked at us after our bad kitchen haircuts and declared us weak, just as he'd been after his mane was shorn.

But really, it was the opposite. When we lost our long hair, AK Akka became surer of herself. She made the water hotter when she washed her face, relished the sting of toner. It's when people think you're weak that you attack, she told me.

So really: Is it a blessing to be pretty?

It was Angel who had told us about blessings, who tried to teach us to speak in her heavenly language. She could speak in tongues. We had learned about blessings at school as well, but they were angrier. In the hallway of St. Laurence O'Toole, for instance, there was a painting of Jesus. Everywhere you stood his eyes were looking at you. You couldn't escape his gaze. His teachings were the things you shouldn't do, and under his gaze, we were inherently sinners. At confession on Fridays, I would lie about what my sins for the week had been. I felt light when all I had to do was an Act of Contrition and some Hail Marys.

But for Angel, it was different. She could say a prayer at the drop of a hat. She prayed over candies we stole from the Mini-Mart. She prayed over the body of a baby squirrel we found puffed up and gray on the sidewalk. She prayed over the note we forged and handed to the clerk at the Mini-Mart, granting Angel permission to buy her aunt cigarettes. And not just any cigarettes—Capri cigarettes, lady cigarettes, fine and thin, not the thick nubs my uncle smoked. We smoked them down by the creek. Angel prayed over our picnics, our lemonade stands, our dolls. She had learned how to pray when her family lived in Missouri, at a Bible camp that my mother said was a cult. They'd been gone for almost two years, but the previous spring, her whole family had limped back to live next door at her aunt's. I'd known she'd returned when I heard her shrill howl of gibberish intermixed with the sound of the chickadees.

Chick-a-zee-zee-zee, the birds would sing.

"Dayo, mbataford, ohjeepa, cadillaca!" Angel would call out from the lawn.

Good morning, America! the mountain chickadee would say, greeting the day.

"Hello, Lord!" Angel said in the beginning.

When Angel spoke like that, I listened. Every day I heard a language I did not understand. Tamil flew around the house like birds. Why was Angel's language any different? And it seemed to me full of blessings. Full of possibility that what we knew could be transformed.

But AK Akka laughed, told Angel to stop, that she knew Angel didn't really know any special language. It was hard, I guess, to believe her; whenever we implored

Angel to speak on command in her heavenly tongue, she balked and began listing car names, adding an *a* or *o* to make them sound exotic. *Chevroletta, Fordo, Oldsmobilea.* We didn't have the heart to challenge her. Once she'd worked through the cars, she'd move on to the spices. *Oreganoa, cinnamonuuu, marjorama, nutmega.*

Ryan, as Angel called Narayan, didn't say a word when Angel would go on like this, just looked at her with a kind of awe. He followed her wherever she went. Narayan was twelve then, and I was nearly twelve too, but AK Akka and Angel were thirteen, Angel close to fourteen. Angel had a sister and brother, Sonata and Bison—they were twins and, at eight, could neither ride bikes nor smoke. They weren't allowed into their aunt's garage, which was where we'd hang out; we'd turn on the radio and roller-skate in circles until one of the adults came home and had to pull in their car. Narayan loved that at their house there was always a pitcher of Kool-Aid. Angel often had a red ring around her mouth. A Kool-Aid mustache. For Narayan, he could drink all he wanted, there was no evidence of it. Our skin stayed brown.

That month was all about objects flying and miracles. Less than a week after our throats were blessed, Halley's Comet reached its perihelion—the closest it got to the sun, the point at which it's easiest to see from Earth.

The comet came every seventy-five years. Its trip into the inner solar system was brief; after just a month, it would leave, slip out between the orbits of Mercury and Venus and disappear into the outer solar system. We had prepared all fall for it. They even said a prayer in Mass for the comet.

Finally, the month had arrived.

My uncle had gotten a job working the graveyard shift at the concrete factory by then—he'd come home early in the morning after clocking out, the house quiet. It was still dark at that time of year, and he'd often stand on our porch, smoking before coming inside, looking at the sky. But that month when the comet was supposed to arrive, he would shower quickly and get his binoculars, then shake us all awake. We'd go out in the morning twilight, while the rest of the house was asleep, and scan the sky. Narayan had a cheap telescope that he'd gotten for Christmas. So far, we'd used it only to spy on the Moores.

It was the quietest time with my uncle. After school, the TV would be blaring, the house full of sunlight, and there were too many doors for him to hide behind. But when we were with him outside, I knew he couldn't hurt us. It was the only time when I felt safe with him.

"It's below Saturn and Mars," he'd say, pointing to the southeast, at the lightening sky. He'd tell us that Jesus once saw Halley's Comet, list off others who might have seen it throughout history. Shakespeare, Dickens, Lincoln. He made up people to entertain us while we stood freezing in the snow.

He too had spent months preparing for the comet. He had me check out books from the school library, simple books on astronomy. I stole an issue of *National Geographic* from the dentist so we could read the feature story about the comet; he turned down the corners of nearly every page. Of the two of them, Auntie Devi was the actual engineer and knew her science. She was supposed to stop working when she'd married, but in India, Vinny Uncle hadn't been able to hold down a job. He'd worked at Thomas Ayyar's match factory, in various positions my great-grandfather gave him after he'd bungled the previous, but eventually he was fired when there was nowhere else to move him. So Auntie Devi had continued to work in India, and now in the US. Free of a mother-in-law, Auntie Devi had run her house in Madras with precision. Vinny Uncle was often out—who knew where—and she was happy about that. When he came home, he smelled of Haywards beer and Gold Flakes. Who needed him? Her sister, Amita, watched Narayan, and then later her mother did. When Devi came home from work, she and her sister would play carrom and take tea. Her mother would cook and they'd watch *Oliyum Oliyum*.

When Amma wrote to tell Vinny Uncle that she

would sponsor him, Auntie Devi had balked. She came to Wyoming only for Narayan. She wanted him to have the choices that she had not. She wanted him to go to college in the US of A and be a doctor.

In Marley, Auntie Devi got a job at Gibson's. She could arrange groceries in a bag like no other. She also made the laciest dosas, though she told us her mother could make even lacier ones. Every time a blue airmail letter arrived from her amma, she tucked it into the pocket of her cardigan and would be sad for days.

She never came out with us to look for the comet. But we never saw it anyway. We had no idea that no matter how long we waited, no matter how early we got up, how clear the sky, we would never see it. That year, the comet and Earth were on opposite sides of the sun; it was one of the worst viewings in the past two thousand years. The only time I was able to see it at all was on a class field trip to the planetarium. There, sitting back in a plush chair, I watched Halley's Comet move across the domed-screen sky again and again. It was beautiful. Bright. Big. It was also fake.

On the last morning that we looked for the comet, we ate breakfast before we went outside. A feast of toast and Tang. Vinny Uncle changed into the fancy knit sweater and slacks he wore to church. Narayan and I put on our school uniforms, as we didn't have anything else that was clean. Agatha Krishna slept in.

Narayan had been up for hours already by the time I came to the table to eat. He had a paper route, delivered the *Marley Tribune* every morning. In the summer, he rode his bike, but in the winter, he put on layer after layer before walking down the unshoveled sidewalks to deliver the news.

When he came to collect for the paper, people always made him talk. They loved his funny accent. "Say 'Welcome,'" they would demand. They delighted in his voice. In his language. He didn't know. "*Velcome.*"

Maybe that was why he and Angel got on so well. People laughed at both of them. Angel had briefly attended our school that spring. Her mother and father had gone back to Missouri, and her aunt had enrolled the lot of them. But Angel had lasted only a month there before she was sent back to the local elementary school. Her theology did not match St. Laurence O'Toole's. Sister St. Luke said she was full of sass. The other girls said she was crazy.

Narayan collected money from everyone in the neighborhood. He once had a Vietnam vet show him the ear that he'd cut off a Vietcong. He kept it wrapped in a handkerchief. Narayan said it looked like dried mango. He collected at the Willow Acres trailer court, where he gathered cans too. He and Vinny Uncle would stomp them flat, then take them to recycling, trading them in for money to spend on McDonald's and pay-per-view boxing.

"This is once in a lifetime," Vinny Uncle said, as we stood in the street, waiting for the comet. He'd said the same thing about Publishers Clearing House and also about a Mötley Crüe concert he'd wanted to go to the previous summer that my mother had nixed because she thought it was satanic. He'd said it about a car too, an old Chevy Impala he'd wanted to buy but didn't have the money for. It was what he'd said when he'd first arrived in America.

For me, though, the comet would likely be twice in a lifetime. When it next appeared in 2061, I would be eighty-eight.

But I knew it would be once in a lifetime for him, and that was why we waited. As we stood, I held a snowball I'd scooped up from the ground, watched it dissolve into water and dirt in my hands, which were so cold I couldn't even open them anymore. The time passed and it became day, but still we stood fast, squinting into the risen sun.

We never saw the comet. And Vinny Uncle would be dead by August. Not all once-in-a-lifetime opportunities are meant to be.

HOW DO YOU KNOW IF
A BOY LIKES YOU?

Have you ever thought a guy might like you but you want to be sure? Take this quiz to see if you're just friends or if he's true-love material!

1. **What does he do if he's sitting next to you in class?**
   a. He asks to borrow a pencil.
   b. He finds an excuse to touch you.
   c. He talks about the latest episode of *The Cosby Show*.
   d. He ignores you.

2. **How does he act at a football game?**
   a. He seems nervous! He sends a friend over to talk to you.
   b. He laughs at your jokes and looks you in the eye.
   c. He acts normal—you're just one of the guys.
   d. He sits with his friends and never looks your way.

3. How often does he initiate conversation?

    a. Seldom—he waits for you to talk first.

    b. Often—he finds reasons to talk to you, mostly about *The Cosby Show*! And *Punky Brewster*!

    c. Sometimes—only if there's something he needs to say.

    d. You are his partner in science lab! That's where you talk.

4. Does he give you compliments?

    a. Not really, but he does like your new Swatch.

    b. Yes! He frequently praises your new mechanical pencil and Trapper Keeper. And your new hair!

    c. Not really; he seems pretty uninterested.

    d. He gives everyone compliments! Even the teacher!

5. When you're in a group, how does he behave around you?

    a. He's the center of attention! There's a reason he's the class clown.

    b. He looks for ways to sit next to you.

    c. What group? You don't hang out outside of class.

    d. He's friendly with everyone. There's a reason he's the most popular.

ANSWERS

Mostly a: Sounds like he might be confused—and not boy-friend material! Tell him to grow up!

Mostly b: If he breaks the barrier of touch, if he finds any excuse to touch you, safe to say he definitely likes you! He knows how to make you center stage!

Mostly c: This guy is your friend and will stay that way. Find someone who puts you first!

Mostly d: This kind of guy loves everyone. He's not your true love.

5

MARCH

I had a farm in Africa. We said that over and over in those first months of the year. We'd all gone to see *Out of Africa.* We'd all watched Amma cry, had stayed up late to watch it win Best Picture. We'd felt so sad knowing that Karen, Meryl Streep's character, would never get even one decent coffee crop from the land. Her soil was no good. Her farm was too high. The rains didn't come. It was a problem we saw all the time. Life was hard. Oil prices were still *down, down, down,* and my father was home *more, more, more.* We knew ranchers who had lost calves in a big spring freeze. We'd seen crops fail. Prices fall. It was the way of the world.

Thomas Ayyar had had a farm in Kerala. Near Kottarakkara. He bought it in his fifties, after becoming a widower. He'd wanted to live out his years in grief as a hermit. He wore white like Gandhi and named the house Gloria Villas in memory of his wife, who had died of untreated diabetes. The house was old, made of stone, with a tiled roof built in a square. It had a large veranda in the front and a spacious main room in the middle. Vinny Uncle and Amma stayed there every summer to escape the Madras heat. All the boy cousins would sleep on the veranda, and the girl cousins slept in the main room. Thomas Thatha had his own bedroom, where he wrote his letters and read his Esperanto texts and his Bible every day.

The house was near the Nilgiri Hills, but everyone called them the Blue Mountains; in a certain light, that was how they appeared, not to mention that every twelve years the light-blue Kurinji flower bloomed all across the slopes. The first major British hill stations were in the Nilgiris, where soldiers, settlers, and colonial officers stayed for relief from the heat of the South Indian plains. They went to Ooty and its tea plantations, where the game of snooker was invented, its rules and practices developed by a certain Sir Neville Chamberlain, no relation to the prime minister. They didn't play carrom, which, like pool, is a strike-and-pocket game. They drank gin and tonics more than the tea from the plantations around them. The officers received gin as part of their rations. They thought they were avoiding malaria, but there are so many ways for the body to get sick. And not all medicine can save you.

Before British rule, the land was owned by the Travancore royal family and was part of the kingdom of Travancore, and then it was a princely state under the British. Amma had a recipe for lime pickle that had been passed down from the royal family's former cook. The secret ingredient was a little bit of jaggery. Whenever she'd make it, we'd eat it with peanut butter on white bread.

The house was surrounded by vegetation, huge eucalyptus trees lining the back, mango trees, rubber trees, cashew nut trees, and coconut palms. Thatha grew pineapples and jackfruit, and a pride of India too, with its bright pink flowers and narcotic seeds.

But above all, Thomas Thatha loved his roses. He grafted roses and studied the gardens of England to see which ones he could grow in his hills. The front of the house flourished with hybrid tea roses called Indian Summer, polyanthus called Rashmi, fairy roses, Pink Parfait grandiflora, a climbing rose called the May Queen, and a white shrub rose called Iceberg. He wrote about his roses in Esperanto to Mr. Clay.

Mr. Clay was a teacher and lived near Windermere, in a town called Hawkshead. William Wordsworth himself had been a student at Hawkshead Grammar School. Thatha almost named the Kottarakkara house Hawks Cottage in honor of Mr. Clay but decided instead to name it after my great-grandmother. There were no hawks on the farm. But Amma said that, once, they ate a bat. A fruit bat their cousin Joseph caught and then cooked as a dry fry.

We knew Wordsworth well: Amma had made us memorize "I Wandered Lonely as a Cloud" and would pay us to recite it to her. She'd had to memorize it herself at Doveton, then spent months wondering what a daffodil was. When she finally saw them, years later, as a student in England, she did indeed find them to be jocund company, so much so that she planted hundreds of bulbs in our yard during our first fall at Cottonwood Cross, when I was a baby and AK Akka a toddler. My father was away on a rig. She sat us in the yard and *dug, dug, dug.* Trumpet cups called Spellbinders and Moonmist, triandrus like Lemon Heart and Liberty Bells. So many wonderful names: Merry Widow, Foggy Dew, Bit o' Gold, Sundial, and Easter Bonnet. Every spring thereafter, they'd come up through the snow, and every spring thereafter, the frost would kill them before they bloomed.

Amma also had been taught by her Anglo-Indian teachers how to make calf's-foot jelly, a mustard poultice, and a Madeira cake, even though she had no oven at home. She learned how to whip eggs and make a blancmange and bananas Foster, which she taught us to make too—AK Akka loved setting things on fire. Before Vinny Uncle lived with us, when it was often just Amma and me and Agatha Krishna, when my father was gone for weeks at a time on rigs, we would make things like floating islands and eat artichokes dipped in butter. We'd stay in our nightgowns all day, and Amma would stand on the heating register, her nightgown puffed up like a bell, and tell us stories about her time at Gloria Villas.

She'd tell us about how at night, she and her cousins would read the Bible and put on theatricals. Amma made all the cousins act out *Goblin Market*. A poem of love and trickery. Vinny Uncle a goblin; Amma, Lizzie.

"Come buy, come buy."

It was the first lesson of the Bible—don't take the fruit. But one of the sisters eats it anyway. The other eats nothing.

At the start of every summer, their athai, Thatha's sister, would gather the children, all the cousins, Amma, and Vinny Uncle. She would lay a clean white sheet out in front of them and draw a scene on it with marker. Every year it was different. A city, a market, a forest. Then she'd take out an old biscuit tin filled with thread and teach the children to embroider the scene. By the end of the summer, the tapestry would be complete and their athai would take it back to Nagercoil, very near the very tip of India.

How we longed to see those sheets. To see any evidence of their life in India. We had almost nothing of Amma's life before Cottonwood Cross.

I did a cross-stitch of a koala for my 4-H club, the Silver Spurs. I suspected that being a woman had a lot to do with cloth. The dove-in-the-window quilt, the drape of a sari, the bandanna that Agatha Krishna stuffed down her underwear, the curtain that Auntie Devi never opened in her room. But I wished we had something like that sheet. Something to show our stories. But instead, we had Agatha Krishna's plays:

JUST SAY NO

AK AKKA: Would you like some candy?

NARAYAN: We're not supposed to take candy from strangers!

GEORGIE: What kind of candy is it?

AK AKKA: Try it! You'll like it.

GEORGIE: I think we can trust her!

NARAYAN: I'm not so sure about this.

(*The kids take the candy.*)

AK AKKA: Psych! That wasn't candy, it was drugs!

NARAYAN: I knew it!

GEORGIE: I don't feel so good.

ANGEL, APPEARING FROM THE WINGS: This could happen to you too! Just say NO to drugs!

ONLY YOU CAN PREVENT FOREST FIRES

GEORGIE: I love playing with matches. Especially here.

NARAYAN: We should be careful. We're on the mountain!

GEORGIE: But a nice fire will warm us up! We can have marshmallows!

NARAYAN: Okay, fine.

ANGEL: Oh, dear! I'm just a deer! But these humans have dropped a match!

NARAYAN: A fire! It's out of control!

(Georgie takes off her coat. She waves it like a flag hitting the ground.)

GEORGIE: Whew! That was close! We could have killed Bambi!

AK AKKA: That *was* close! ONLY YOU CAN PREVENT FOREST FIRES!

We had many variations on the theme. Sometimes AK Akka was a satanist. Other times she made us play nuclear war. All the plays involved saving ourselves after we'd acted with poor judgment. St. Laurence O'Toole told us that every Friday in Mass—we could always be saved. Father Duffy also told us Jesus *always* forgives. There was nothing we could do that would make Jesus not love us.

We told stories like Karen Blixen in *Out of Africa*. Like Isak Dinesen. She had two names too. AK Akka had memorized the scene from the movie where Karen's at a table with a bunch of white men. They give her a line, and she has to build a story from it to entertain them. You could almost feel sorry for her being a colonist. Because even as a colonist, she had to perform for the men. AK Akka told me not to feel bad for her or her crops though. She shouldn't have been there in the first place.

> *There was a wandering Chinese named Cheng Huan*
> *Living in Limehouse*
> *And a girl named Shirley*
> *Who spoke perfect Chinese*
> *Which she learned from her missionary parents*
> *Cheng Huan lived alone in a room on Formosa Street*
> *   above the Blue Lantern*
> *He sat at his window, and in his poor listening heart*
> *Strange echoes of his home and country*

AK Akka would put a flower in her hair, hold an empty wineglass, and tell us her own stories.

> *There was an Indian girl*
> *Living in Cottonwood Cross*
> *And an* other *girl*

Who did not speak Tamil
Which they did not learn because it was confusing
The girls lived with their family on Kit Carson Drive
     near the Mini-Mart
They sat at the window, and in their poor listening
     hearts
Strange echoes of their home and country

Karen Blixen's African farm always reminded Amma of the Kottarakkara house. The dark wood furniture. The candlelight. The mosquito nets on the beds. The cuckoo clock. Did Amma see herself like Karen Blixen? Trying to make a home in a place that would fail you? We weren't supposed to like her, this white woman. But Karen Blixen was split in two as well, I think. There would always be one part of her in Africa, one in Denmark. And she knew about bad men too. Her man, Denys Finch Hatton, was a big-game hunter, and from what we knew of being hunted indoors, we knew he must be no good.

In the Kottarakkara house, all the cousins would sing "Poor Papa." I loved the lyrics. The way that Mama got to eat and wear diamonds. In that song, the men starved.

Everyone cheers when Mama appears
She's got diamonds stuck in her ears

But poor Papa, poor Papa
He's got nothing at all

And Mama eats ham, and Mama eats lamb
Mama eats bread with strawberry jam
But poor Papa, poor Papa
He eats nothing at all

Amma taught it to us one day when we had a wet spring snow that snapped the power lines in two. She made a fire and roasted hot dogs over the flames with chopsticks. Vinny Uncle was sleeping. Auntie Devi was at work. We wrapped ourselves in sleeping bags. Narayan sang the loudest of us all, his thumbs hooked under imaginary suspenders as he marched through the house. Vinny Uncle woke up and joined us. He and Amma sang loud and clear. All of us danced. And then Agatha Krishna switched to "Holiday." Her hair had started to grow back, and she was trying to style it like Madonna's. We all laughed.

But most days, we were in a house of women. Most days we felt the chill air between Amma and Auntie Devi. The only songs were the ones that Agatha Krishna tried to record off the radio with her tape deck.

After Vinny Uncle died, we never sang like that again. Our fathers were gone—one dead, one on the rigs. Poor, poor papas.

6

IT

Why kill a man? you ask.

Why would you kill your very own special uncle?

All right, I'll finally tell you.

It's like freeze tag.

For a game that seems like chaos, freeze tag has a lot of rules. First, there are the boundaries. The game is played to the west, from the Moores' driveway to the edge of the lawn of the neighbors you don't know, and then to the east, from your lawn to the house of the neighbors you never see. The safe zone is a large cottonwood tree in the middle of the lawn, technically yours, but it's the Moores who trim the branches every year. The tree is large and when you hit the trunk and yell "safe," it marks your hands with mottled impressions like an orange. It's fissured, has canker in its trunk; the tree is diseased.

You hate being It. Chasing people all over the lawn,

waiting while everyone else keeps one hand on the tree, as far away from you as possible. You don't have the energy to pursue them. To catch the others. You prefer being in the game, running away yourself, waiting till It is out of sight before darting across the lawn to the borders of each driveway.

The rules say that if you're tagged, you have to freeze. There's an art to freezing. You have to strike an exaggerated pose, as if you were caught mid-stride, holding a foot in the air, half jumping; one girl tries to freeze in a cartwheel. But when you're tagged yourself, you just stand there, waiting for someone to run by and slap you on the back, to tell you that you're safe. You seem always to be waiting, watching the game around you, never really in it but never really out of it either.

That's how it feels with Vinny Uncle too—remember? You're out of your body, looking down. You're split in two. There's a you and a me. The you lies there, frozen, as horrible things happen to her. The me is up above, watching. If you ever want to be whole again, you have to bring the two parts together.

In the moment, though, you take in the smell of cigarettes, the blare of the TV outside the bathroom. You can hear a boxing match. But you are not you; you're the frozen you. And you stay frozen.

Narayan once told you that if you're being attacked by a bear, it's best to play dead; eventually the bear will grow bored, let you go. So you try that. The first time you're in the bathroom, you don't fight at all. You watch your body from above; you play dead. When you go back to your bedroom, you can tell that AK Akka knows. She knows what happened in the bathroom because her self was split there too.

The second time, you think you really might be dead. You still haven't tried to fight him. You're limp and pliable. But he doesn't grow bored, not either time, doesn't walk away; he only gets bolder. And the truth is, as awful as it is, it also doesn't feel bad. And he tells you it's okay.

You just don't like it when he takes his penis out. You thought you knew about sex, that it wouldn't be so bad. You have a babysitter who knows how to put tooth-picks in the cable box to watch the Playboy channel, so you've seen things. But this isn't what you expected. This looks like a burnt hot dog, and when he puts your hand to it, you can feel something alive.

And it feels like freeze tag. A game you now hate. You're always slapped early. You have to stand, fro-zen in the crabgrass, watching the others play around you, waiting for someone to come by and free you. For someone to yell "you're safe."

And you think that is how you will be saved—by someone else.

One afternoon, when you can taste tobacco in your

mouth, you run to your shared bedroom and slap her with all your might. She knows what it feels to be out of body. To have something happen that you don't know how to freeze. Your hand makes contact with her back, and you scream, "Safe!" You grab her by the arm and take her to the climbing tree outside, where you both sit, frozen, waiting for someone to find you, for someone to save you from the game you don't know how to save yourselves from.

But Amma isn't going to fix this. He's made sure of that. He's told you they will all go back to India if you tell. That Amma will have no family. That Narayan won't go to college. And that he will deny it.

And you know how lonely Amma was before.

So no one will come. No one can remove you from this game. Only you can take the me and the you and put them back together. Only you can save yourself.

7

YOU

You're uncomfortable now.
   I'm sorry.

8

YOU

You're uncomfortable now.
    I'm not sorry.

9

APRIL

Dear Joy,

I'm sorry I still haven't sent you any candy. Pen pal fail. And my mom says I can't call you either. It's too expensive. My grandparents in India are dead, but my great-grandfather is very old and alive. My mom calls him even though it's very expensive. He writes her long letters on thin blue paper. You have to open the letters carefully so you don't cut through the middle of the letter. He wants my mother and uncle to send him seeds. And he wants a bottle of Jack Daniel's. But I don't think you can send that. I hate my uncle and his family. They took my sister's room when they moved here, so now we have to share. It was supposed to be temporary, but they don't have enough money for an apartment. And my uncle watches us for free while my mom and Aunt Devi work. My uncle married my aunt for a motor scooter. She made him sell it later. They had an arranged marriage. My parents didn't. They met at a party. My dad is white. He's gone a lot. On oil rigs. I look up the price of oil in the paper every day. I also follow stocks. My dad says if oil gets to be over fifty dollars a barrel, we'll have the biggest party.

My uncle doesn't really watch us anyway. He just watches TV and smokes. He loves us very much. Too much. I smoke too. Capris. My best friend, Angel, gets them for me. Angel knows when people are satanists. Are there satanists in Africa?

Yours till the candle sticks,
Georgie

Dear Joy,

I hate my life. I hate my parents. They're so mean. They don't let me go anywhere. They won't let me spend the night at my friend Heather's. They say they don't know her parents. And that her father has too many guns. Your parents seem cool. My parents hate Bon Jovi and Def Leppard or anything cool. Did you hear about Chernobyl? Did you see the movie *The Day After*? My mom taped it. I'm so scared of nuclear war. There's a missile base in Wyoming. What if Russia wants to kill us? I think about being dead sometimes.

Yours till Niagara Falls,
Georgie

Dear Joy,

Have you seen *The Little Princess*? It's one of my favorite movies. My sister and I like to pretend that we're Becky and Sara Crewe, locked in our attic room.

I like that Sara likes India. But then she's forced to go to boarding school in cold England. But even in England there's Ram Dass. The Indian servant of the old man next door. He's very kind to Sara. Even when she isn't a princess anymore. It's like in *Annie* too. In *Annie*, there's Punjab. He also worked with an old white man. Daddy Warbucks. Punjab saved Annie. Ram Dass saved Sara. They both wore turbans.

The only Indian man I really know is my uncle, and he isn't like them at all.

LYLAS,
Georgie

Dear Joy,

[I want to say: *Help me.*] I liked the stamps on your last letter. [*Help me.*]

[*Help.*] I have read all the Famous Five. Anne is my favorite. [*Help me.*] What a lot of adventures! [*Help me.*] We don't have anything like that here. [*Do we?*] A policeman came to our school today to talk about Satan. He told us there are people who sacrifice cats. Our neighbor's cat was poisoned. It ate antifreeze.

[*Can't help him.*] He said satanists hide in plain sight. Practicing spells and evil. You don't know how evil people can be. [*Punjab, help me! Ram Dass, help me!*] I'm sorry I still haven't sent the candy. [*Help me.*]

KIT,

Georgie

HOW DO YOU KNOW IF YOU'RE READY TO HAVE A SEXUAL RELATIONSHIP?

1. **Are you making your own decisions about when to start a sexual relationship, or are other people influencing your choices?**
   a. All me. I don't feel any pressure from my partner or others.
   b. Other people. My partner and friends put a lot of pressure on me.

2. **Are you choosing to have sex for the correct reasons?**
   a. Yes. I want to have sex because I feel ready, both my body and mind are at peace, and my partner is someone I connect with.
   b. No. I'm choosing to have sex because I feel pressure and I want to make my partner happy. Sex is the only way to improve my relationship with my partner.

3. **Do you know how to avoid sexually transmitted diseases and unwanted pregnancy?**
   a. Yes. I have studied sex education and know how my body works.
   b. No. I have no knowledge besides what I've seen on TV.

4. **Do you feel your partner would respect your decision, whether you choose to have sex or not?**
   a. Yes. My partner would respect my decision no matter what.
   b. No. My partner might not respect my decision if I choose not to have sex.

ANSWERS

Mostly a: You are ready. Sex is a serious but beautiful part of any healthy couple's relationship. It sounds like you and your partner have open lines of communication! You're in it to win it!

Mostly b: Not so much. You might want to rethink your partner and your choices. Communication is the key to any relationship. Girlfriend, there are more fish in the sea!

10

MAY

On May Day we leave flowers on the porches of every house on Kit Carson. We saved strawberry baskets all year to put them in, little green baskets that we fill with beds of old Easter grass, crepe paper flowers, and hyacinths that we picked from the yard.

Amma went to Oxford. Back in the day, she was going places. She told us that in Oxford, May Day morning is a really big deal. It begins at sunrise as a choir greets the day with a chorus of hymns. There are Morris dancers who perform near the Radcliffe Camera. And anyone who's still awake from the balls the night before jumps into the Isis River. They don't even mind ruining their dresses.

Mayday!

In Oxford, Amma wore a gown. It wasn't really a proper gown, more like a black vest. It had cigarette holes—Amma smoked then and would sometimes be so deep in conversation she didn't notice her cigarette burning a hole right through her clothes.

She still has the gown, and we wear it whenever we play court. Before a hanging at the big cottonwood tree, AK Akka or Angel puts it on and bangs the pestle from the kitchen. The pestle smells of garlic and coriander. They *bang, bang, bang* while a prisoner pleads for their life. I wish we could put on the gown and call Vinny Uncle outside to the cottonwood. But he sleeps all day long.

Mayday, Mayday!

Agatha Krishna began bleeding at the beginning of May. She had spotted before, but this was the first big bleed. She put her hands down her pants and felt blood. We knew what that meant—we'd read *Are You There, God? It's Me, Margaret*. In that book they had to wear belts, but now there are pads that stick right to your underwear. Amma told us that in Kottarakkara, all the girl cousins would get their periods at the same time. There was one privy, where they all would wash out their rags. She said it was a mess. Here at least it's neat, and no one sees.

It stopped Vinny Uncle though. After that, all his attention was on me. We said little to each other about him. AK Akka was done with his hands, done with them on her, and done with them on me. We tried to move out of the house. It was still cold, but AK Akka set up our tent in the yard. I was going to summer camp the next month and had a new sleeping bag. We moved all our bedding into the tent. We told Amma we wanted to sleep outside, even though it was so cold, there was frost on the rain fly. We huddled against each other all night long, while Narayan slept in our room. We shared a flashlight and flipped through magazines until we fell asleep. Sometimes we would zip our sleeping bags together to make one big pocket. And AK Akka would whisper in my ear, going over what we needed to do.

Mayday, Mayday, Mayday!
NATURE OF EMERGENCY: Vinny Uncle!

Amma told AK Akka that she had to have a ceremony to mark becoming a woman. It's what Brahmins do, Ritusuddhi. I had thought for a long time that we were of no caste, since we're Christian, but we were, and some Brahmins mark being a woman.

Is that even true? Who knows. We never had anyone to fact-check anything about our Indianness with.

Caste no bar! Wheatish complexion! Homely! Foreign-returned!

The other Indians we know? A strange menagerie. There are two doctors who work at the hospital. A nephrologist and an allergist. There's an engineer and his family. There's an architect, a motel owner. There are other others who come and go over the years; I don't know what they all do. They only show up for one party, then we never see them again. And, of course, everyone speaks a different language, and so we all end up speaking English. If only we all spoke Esperanto! In the house, Appa, AK Akka, and I are the ones who don't speak Tamil. When Auntie Devi and Amma argue, when Amma tells Vinny Uncle what to do, I can't understand what they're talking about. It all sounds fast and angry. When we ask Appa what's going on, he tells us that Amma thinks that—as the older sister, and since it's her house—she should be able to make all the rules. All we really know is that Auntie Devi spends a lot of time alone in her room while Amma and Vinny Uncle take tea and laugh at the kitchen table.

There's an Indian party every few months. Someone drives to Denver for supplies: sacks of rice, dal, mustard seed, cumin, urad dal, jars of pickle, turmeric, snack bags of mixture. Once in a while, someone will find fresh vegetables—eggplants the size of golf balls, bitter melon, or drumstick. It is broadly understood that if you go to Denver, you're buying for the group.

At the parties, everyone wears saris and kurtas. There's always film music playing. We eat the kinds of food that take too long to make for us to eat every day. Puris. Rasmalai. Jalebis. There are always gulab jamun, which Amma makes from Bisquick. There's always an open packet of Danish butter cookies. We drink real chai, and Amma and Auntie Devi drink sherry. The men drink whisky. Vinny Uncle always gets drunk, and when he's drunk, he's angry. Those are the worst nights. If Appa is away, we go sleep with Amma to keep safe.

Mayday! Altitude, 5,118 feet!

Agatha Krishna didn't really care about having a party; she said she didn't really have a caste, no matter what Amma said. But she did want the presents. So she went along with it. She'd wear her first sari, get her first gold jewelry, though she'd also have to drink raw egg every day for sixteen days ahead of time, and then have a ritual oil bath. Amma joked that if we were in Kottarakkara, AK Akka would have to sit on a chair outside so that everyone would know she was ready for marriage offers.

Poor AK Akka. She didn't ever want to be married. But I knew that she had a secret boyfriend. Jason Parks. He played basketball and had a sister in my class, Claudette. AK Akka and Jason ate lunch together, and sometimes after school they'd go to the Mini-Mart and he'd buy her a pop and some penny candies. She'd bring home candy for Narayan and me as long as we didn't tell Amma that she was hanging out with Jason. He once gave her a heart-shaped locket.

I told AK Akka that she should sleep in the tent. In India, they make women go to little huts when they're on their period because they're considered unclean. But

AK Akka is so very clean. She has Noxzema. She has Sea Breeze. And we were already sleeping in the tent anyway, away from everyone. Her period just made it easier to explain why we didn't want to be in the house.

Amma and Appa had to go to the mall to buy AK Akka her first piece of gold jewelry. The beginning of her dowry. My father didn't pay a dowry for Amma, and now oil prices are *down, down, down*. But they thought that Agatha Krishna should have some gold anyway. A small set from Zales. Earrings and a necklace like a flower.

The mall is my most favorite place in the world. Everything is ordered and clean. There are security guards who make sure you're safe. If you're lost, there's an office where you can go and a nice lady will hold your hand and wait with you for Amma to come.

And then there's the food—it all smells so good. Hot dogs on a stick. Cotton candy. Java Jitters. A whole shop for coffee! Orange drinks whipped so light, so different from the concentrate that we have in the freezer, which is thick with syrup.

The mall arcade is called Aladdin's Castle. It's dark, and Narayan spends hours in there, playing *Pac-Man* and *Super Mario Bros.* Appa loves Narayan. Narayan asks him about geology, and Appa gets out his microscope to show Narayan soil samples. He gifted him an arrowhead he found and gives Narayan a heavy roll of quarters once a month. Narayan spends some of them at the arcade and some on Archie Comics. In India, he had more than one hundred Archies. He tells me about his India often. How his paati, Auntie Devi's mom, would feed him with her hands. She'd make balls out of curry and rice and drop them into his mouth. He played cricket on the street, and at night he and his amma would sleep on the terrace on the roof. He missed India a lot. But they didn't have arcades there like the one at the mall.

There's also a photo booth where you can get pictures of yourself taken in one long strip. I asked Heather Ross to be in a photo strip with me, but she said no. So I just took photos of myself instead. I stuck out my tongue. I pretended to cry. I crossed my eyes. I photographed my face again and again. AK Akka has a photo of her and Jason Parks. She keeps it in her Bible.

I don't have much money, but when I went with Amma and Appa to get AK Akka's gold jewelry, I bought myself a small bag of cola gummy bottles, some stickers of hearts and little hats, and jelly bracelets. Later that summer, I got myself the new Genesis album too.

Listen, you know I love you, but I just can't take this.

One of my favorite stores at the mall is the one where you can get a T-shirt with your name on it. Your own *exotic* name, in velvet letters across any design.

Rainbows. Your favorite band. A Wyoming scene: mountains, Yellowstone, Devils Tower. (Years from now, tribes will want to call Devils Tower something else: *Bear Lodge*.) The magic of the T-shirt place is that, with just the press of an iron, you can finally have your own branded thing, even if you gave up on ever seeing your name on mini license plates or necklaces a long time ago.

You know I want to, but I'm in too deep.

The mall is also the most diverse place in Marley.

It is the West, after all, and to go west you need work. To be a pioneer, you need to be able to make your fortune.

Just outside the mall is a motel run by an Indian family. They sell shelter. We met them at Gibson's one day, and they started coming over to the house for our India parties after that.

Inside the mall, there's a girl from Russia who sells Dead Sea salt scrub from a kiosk. She has a sink and washes your hands with the care of a mother.

Next to her is a man from Iran who sells flat irons that will press your hair straight as a bullet.

There's a Vietnamese family that can lacquer and paint anything you want on your nails—an American flag, a flower, even a school mascot.

And then there's the Turkish grain-of-rice man. He can write your name on a single grain of rice. He could even write the Lord's Prayer on a single grain of rice. Or the word *fuck*. No matter what you have him write, though, he'll put the rice in a small glass vial filled with glycerin that can go on a chain—your name, a prayer, or *fuck*, hanging around your neck.

Finally, there's the Chinese couple; they sell food. Orange chicken. Sesame chicken. Fried rice with carrots chopped like blocks and peas like planets, oily, soy-stained, ready to be consumed.

And then: us. Two girls who always come out looking gray when they go to the cosmetics counter of the department store and ask for a makeover. They don't have foundation to match our skin. When Narayan sees us afterward at the food court, he says, "You're turning into ghosts."

Mayday! Emergency!

Home from the mall with supplies in hand, Amma was ready for the party. Auntie Devi and Vinny Uncle gave AK Akka a silver plate filled with fruit: oranges, apples, pears. Plus an envelope with $101 in it. Other people gave her gifts too. The allergist and his wife gave her a set of costume jewelry, the nephrologist a card with a twenty-dollar bill.

It was at the party that we gave Vinny Uncle his first dose. Someone had brought cheap, off-brand soda. Strawberry. Pineapple. Vinny Uncle had a glass of whisky and a glass of soda that he'd drink whenever Amma was nearby. That's what we put the antifreeze in. It was almost too easy.

We didn't yet know how much we could get away with before he'd notice the flavor. We started with just a small amount to test the water. AK Akka had been drinking raw eggs for seven days at that point, so she knew that most people would drink anything if it was put in front of them.

Mayday! Number of people on board, two! No fuel remaining!

Our practice run made him vomit. We felt a little bad when he locked himself in the bathroom. We felt a little bad when Narayan brought him Alka-Seltzer. When Auntie Devi made him rice and curd to soothe his stomach. Amma made him bread with butter and sugar. We felt bad enough that we decided to let him have the summer. He was so excited for the fair. To see Van Halen at the Events Center. He'd been singing "Jump" for months.

So we decided to give him that. The concert. The summer is the best time in Wyoming anyway. I felt relieved when I heard his car through our open window in the morning. Knowing we hadn't done it yet. But then AK Akka would hum the chorus of "The Final Countdown" to remind me that his stay of execution was just temporary. That we needed to give him more.

He drank so much soda. Bright Mountain Dew in big cups. It was surprisingly easy to make him sick. What we were learning was, it was harder to kill him than we'd imagined.

That night, after our first attempt, AK Akka and I went out to our tent and held hands. We held hands so very tightly. We held each other till morning. Till the tent was wet with dew.

Till Vinny Uncle unzipped the door and told us to come inside.

11

CASTE IN THE AMERICAN WEST:
A BRIEF DEPARTURE

Vinny Uncle liked to fish. He also liked to cheat.

Appa liked to fish too. It was the one thing we did alone with him. He would take us out to the North Platte and walk us through the tedium of the activity. We caught very little. But Appa would tell us stories about the rocks around the riverbank. He taught us how to skip stones. He would pick sego lilies and tell us how the Mormons ate them when they were starving on the trail west. He would tie dry flies and teach us how to angle. If we caught rainbow or brown trout, we'd take the whole fish home to Amma. She especially loved the fish heads. She'd fillet the bodies for us in a little butter, salt and pepper, and flour, but for herself, she'd make a fish head curry. Rich in gingelly oil and mustard seeds. Tomatoes and ginger.

When we went fishing with Vinny Uncle, we never

went off the beaten path. We'd park near the road. This was worm fishing. Vinny Uncle would pull a can of sweet corn out of his pocket and use a bottle opener to make two holes in the lid. And then he'd pitch it into the Platte.

"The fish love the corn."

He'd cast to the can, lure the fish to his little honey hole.

This was the kind of cast we heard all about in Wyoming. But I want to tell you about caste. You know one kind of cast. I know two. As I said, caste meant nothing to me. Honestly, I think Amma only did that ceremony for Agatha Krishna because she was bored. She missed home. The caste I grew up on was cast. Boys were taught to fish. Girls were taught to watch. When we went with Vinny Uncle, he only ever talked to Narayan. Even with Appa, once Narayan came, that's who he talked to too. They didn't know they were prepping him to one day pose with a fish on an app to make women swipe right or left. So many of the men around us killed. Deer. Antelope. Pheasants. There was so much posing next to dead, silent creatures.

I see now that caste and cast are really not so different. They both require discipline. They both require money. A world you are born into. Class. Caste. Both hooked us. There is a difference between worm fishing with a can of sweet corn and the spangled art of a fly. Vinny Uncle never had a real cast. You only have to look to Jackson Hole and the fancy fly shops to know that it takes money to fish. To cast out a line with a bit of hair and feathers or even a bit of mink. But both ask you to step into a river. They both ask you to uncover what is beneath the surface. Far from what the eye can see. These are the two worlds I come from. Both are privilege. Both are sleight of hand. Both are choreography.

THE EQUIPMENT

To become a fisherman, and to use fly rod casting, you must have the proper equipment. And that costs. The waders. The vest. And above all, you need a rod. Rods are made of bamboo and graphite. Think of the rod as part of your arm. It converts your intentions into motion. Along with the rod, you need a reel and fly line—the foundation of a successful cast. The fly itself is really an imitation, a decoy to entice the fish to your line.

You are born. Your skin will either be fair and lovely. Or dusky and dark. You cannot do much about that. You need nothing else. You cannot mimic another caste. Your name. Your face. Your job. It is designed for you.

THE PRACTICE

To fish, you must be secure in your footing. Move to a part of the water where your footing is nice and steady and stand with your shoulders and hips in line with your target zone. When angling in swift water, you have to be especially conscious of your body and foot placement. It can be very easy to slip if you're not careful! It's very easy to misstep.

You must position yourself with your feet planted wide. Your shoes, you will take off when you enter the house. But you must not lose your footing. You walk with the step of the righteous. Ignore others who might be on the street. Anyone who eats meat. Who wasn't born with all that you were born with. Do not let them interrupt your stride. Do not allow yourself to be knocked off course. It can be so easy to slip.

1. Hold the rod. Wrap your dominant hand around the handle comfortably.
   Hold the whip. Your dominant hand is your right hand. We do not touch with the left.
2. Form a grip.
   Grip tight. This is your birthright.
3. Hold the line. With your nondominant hand, hold the fly line near the reel. You can use your index finger and middle finger to grip the line.
   Hold the line with your right hand. Your left hand is useless.

4. Strip out the line. Strip out enough line from the reel so you can cast.

   Give some line. It's best that people don't feel tension. It's best if people don't know you are above them.

5. Start the cast.

   You have been one with the caste since the day you came out of your mother.

6. Straighten out the line behind you.

   You must stay on course. You did not start this. Your ancestors did. You just have to walk the line they left for you.

7. Load the rod. Hasten the forward motion of the rod, then stop at the one-o'clock position. Transfer energy to the line and allow it to unfurl in the air.

   Let your power guide you forward. Get the positions you want. Marry well.

8. Release the line from your nondominant hand so that it flies forward. Energy is stored in the rod and you move it.

   You have the energy. You are the only one who can be you. You were chosen.

9. Follow through. Allow the rod to continue its head-long movement.

   It is always forward motion. You cannot control it.

10. Carefully manipulate the amount of line you let out. Your cast will be more accurate this way.

    You control the story.

11. Practice and modify. Repeat. Practice your timing, power, and control. Adjust your method to get better accuracy and distance.

    It may be hard at first. This thing you are born into. That you didn't choose. But the thing is, you did choose it. You did something in a past life to deserve this. You are owed this. You are the reason you have power. So own it.

12. Manipulate the line with soft, gentle motions. You have to present a convincing performance of a fly if you want to catch a fish.

    Manipulate the line. Rule the line. It's your birthright.

And in the end: Remember to pose with your prize. Is it a fish? Is it a marriage? Are they really so different?

12

JUNE

Come June, I'd moved from one tent to another, and Agatha Krishna and I were separated for two weeks. I went to Girl Scouts camp, and she stayed home to play in a summer softball league. At some point that season, she got hit in the face with a softball; her braces were the only thing that kept her front tooth in place. We didn't have health insurance, and my father grumbled over the cost of fixing it. If only we'd known an Indian dentist!

Agatha Krishna had left Girl Scouts the year before. She'd even stopped eating their cookies, opting for celery instead because she'd become obsessed with being thinner. And so I went to the mountain alone. To Camp Sacagawea, née Sacajawea. The name wouldn't be changed until years after I went. And then Sacagawea's whole story would be rewritten.

I was ready to leave the house. The cups of pop.

Sleeping in the tent. Waking up with dew on our shoes. I was tired of Narayan playing Atari and Amma and Auntie Devi fighting. The volume in the whole house had turned up too high.

Camp Sac was on Marley Mountain, which rises to 8,300 feet of elevation. Most of the face of the mountain is covered in lodgepole pines, with their long, straight trunks and bushy arms like cleaning brushes. There are a few aspens too, with their gold-coin leaves, and ponderosas scattered between.

My first day at camp, I met Abby Young, who was raised on a ranch west of town. Her father had home-schooled her until the year before. She taught us all to smell the bark of the ponderosas—her dad ran his cows up Rock Creek Mountain every summer, and that place is thick with ponderosas.

"It smells like butterscotch or caramel, doesn't it?" Abby said. With our noses pressed right up to the trunks, we looked like we were kissing the trees.

Holiday Jones disagreed. "I think it smells like vanilla cake. At my last birthday party, in Hollywood— at a movie studio, mind you—I had a cake made by the same people who make all the celebrity wedding cakes."

"I think it smells like both!" I said. I was used to either/or. To a thing being one thing, then another. To be half, you get used to switching which half you are at any time. I knew all about something being two things. About pleasing people with the right answer.

Holiday picked a flake of bark off her pink fleece.

Poor Abby said nothing. They didn't bake cakes in her house. Her mother was dead. Her dad only bought practical things, like a loaf of bread, milk, apples, frozen mixed vegetables, cereal, and lettuce. They ate their own meat. Occasionally, he'd bring home a large tub of ice cream.

Amma would bring home all sorts of impractical things for us to eat. She fed us spoons of condensed milk. Sometimes she made us cream of mushroom soup with a spoonful of Harveys Bristol Cream in it. Oil was down, but when the supply list for camp arrived, along with a cheery letter from Mrs. Watson, the director, my mother had taken me to the outdoors store and bought everything on it. All new. The store sold guns and orange vests. Deer heads watched us from the walls. Once we'd gotten all my gear home, Amma labeled everything with a big marker, from sleeping bag to bug repellent. I twirled in my new raincoat while she did. With my brown face and yellow slicker, I looked like a sunflower.

"You could survive a monsoon!" Vinny Uncle announced.

"I know how to survive anywhere," I mumbled back.

But Camp Sacajawea was not made to make us survive. It was made to give frazzled parents a break. A place to earn a patch on your sash. It was nothing like *The Parent Trap*. I was in a group with other girls: Kiki Price would be at Camp Sacajawea for two weeks, and then she was off to Vacation Bible School, Camp Faith, for another two. Her father, who only got custody of her in the summer, worked full-time in the oil fields and was rarely home. Kiki's summer was a string of programs. She normally lived in North Dakota. But her mother, who was married to a real estate agent now, was pregnant with twins and wanted some "well-deserved rest." It was her dad's girlfriend, Lydia, who had gone through the supply list for Kiki, calling friends to ask if they had a sleeping bag, a nonbreakable cup. She took Kiki to Big Lots! and bought her a soap on a rope.

"When I went to camp, soap on a rope was a must!" Lydia had told her. But the last thing Kiki had seen hanging from a rope was her cat Cool. The real estate agent had told her he was teaching her a lesson. That talking back didn't fly in his house.

She also knew what it took to survive in a house where strange men had come to stay.

Holiday Jones said she was from Hollywood and that if you could survive an LA freeway, you could survive anywhere. Later, we'd learn that Holiday Jones was not, in fact, from Hollywood. She was from the

Valley, from Van Nuys. Her parents didn't work in the movies, per se. Her dad catered and her mother cut hair—sometimes for minor celebrities.

The other seventy-five campers were a mix, mostly Marley girls, but some stragglers from other parts of the state, plus a few more out-of-towners too, girls whose parents wanted them to have a Western adventure, but who couldn't get them into camps in Jackson Hole or to Cheley in Estes Park. It was all scraps who ended up at Camp Sac, which was technically for Girl Scouts, but times being what they were, any girl who wanted to come was admitted.

Abby, Kiki, Holiday, and I were all in the Alpine Forget-Me-Not group. We were counseled by Mrs. Watson, the camp director, a woman so muscled and wiry, she looked as if she could scale a ponderosa. She wore tinted lenses that turned into sunglasses when she went outside. You could never quite see her eyes. All the other counselors were named things like Cloud, Rain, Juniper, and Willow. But Mrs. Watson was always Mrs. Watson. Our cabin counselor was Sun, but we only really saw her at bedtime and in the morning. She appeared only when Mrs. Watson was around.

After breakfast every day, Mrs. Watson called us around the "circle of trust," a clearing in the woods where downed lodgepole pine trunks had been arranged in a circle.

"Ladies," she told us the first day. "You are the eldest at Camp Sacajawea."

Most of us were barely twelve, except for Abby, who was thirteen, on account of failing second grade years ago. "It will be up to you to carry the torch this year, so to speak, at the end-of-camp pageant."

Abby kicked the ground with her boot. She hadn't brought hiking boots with her, just her lace-up cowboy boots.

"You mean the Lewis-and-Clark thing?"

Mrs. Watson was breathless. "Yes, the dramatic re-telling of how Sacajawea, with a baby on her back, led Lewis and Clark to the ocean, all the while acting as their guide, translating for them across the West."

"I have a lot of dramatic experience," piped up Holiday. "With my hair long and all, I would make a mean Sacajawea." She turned up her face and put her hand to her head. She shook her tangled brown hair out of her baseball cap.

Mrs. Watson squinted at her. "Yes, well, I was thinking, since Georgie here is Indian, she really looks the part. I think she should be our Sacajawea. Holiday, you might make a fine Meriwether Lewis. And, Kiki, perhaps you'd like to be William Clark."

"Whatever." Kiki's blond hair was cut short like a boy's.

"I thought you were Mexican," Holiday said to me.

"I'm Indian." I picked at the pine needles on the ground. I hated saying what I was.

"And Abby. Abby, you're so handy. I know you sew with 4-H, and, of course, you do so much around the ranch. You can make the sets and costumes. I, of course, will direct. And the younger girls will fill in as the various people Lewis and Clark and Sacajawea meet along the way. Some of them can play animals too."

I ran my fingers through my hair and felt for the phantom braids that Amma had cut away months before. I always played a brown girl who people only half believed.

"But enough pageant talk. Abby's been here before; she can walk you through all this later. The only difference is that this year we won't be able to have any candles." Every year after the pageant, there was a ceremonial lighting—candle by candle, from one girl to the next—in honor of the end of camp. "The fire danger's too high, so we'll have to use glow sticks." She held up a thin plastic tube filled with a milky substance that roiled back and forth like a level.

After that, we returned to our bunks to get our backpacks. Our cabins were actually big canvas tents on wooden platforms. We were all crammed into low bunks. I slept in a bunk with Kiki. She was on top.

Come bedtime, I'd lie awake and listen for night-hawks diving for insects, their wings making a *womp* like an alien landing. I slept with the small jar of curry powder that Amma had given me to ward off homesick-ness. When I smelled it, I missed the way the sweat of onions and garlic permeated our house. Auntie Devi and Amma would often compete for our affection with cooking. I was very loyal to Amma, but it was indisput-able that Auntie Devi made the best dosas. Her dosas were like a valentine on a plate. She would pour a little mound of sugar next to the batter, then stick her finger in the middle and pour in some ghee. A lake on the mountain. Ghee and sugar. My fingers sparkling in the morning sun.

The main activity at Camp Sac was finding your way out of the woods. Learning to navigate.

"Ladies," Mrs. Watson said. "You must have your wits about you in the wild. You must know that with simple skills, you can find your way out of anything. Today you're going to learn to orient a map to north, read the symbols in a legend, identify the shapes of dif-ferent geographical features, and interpret topography lines."

She broke us into groups. We were going to be sent out on a course that Mrs. Watson had plotted through the woods and had to make our way back to camp on our own.

We looked to Abby to lead us. She was used to reading maps. She and her father went hunting each fall, and they would spend weeks before their trip planning and marking their base camp. Abby regularly got an antelope. That fall, she was trying for an elk.

"You know, it was Lewis and Clark who first mapped the West," Mrs. Watson said as we got ready to go.

Abby looked at her. "Lewis and Clark didn't even go through Wyoming," she snapped.

"Well, yes, I know that," Mrs. Watson replied, gripping her clipboard tight.

"But you know, some people think that Sacajawea didn't die back east like people have always said. Some people think that she lived out the last of her years in Wyoming, on the Wind River Reservation. They're still trying to prove that, but she was definitely in Wyoming at some point," Abby added.

Holiday studied the map. "There sure isn't any water around here." On the first day of camp, she'd tried on her swimsuit, a bikini, for all of us.

"There's no lakes or anything nearby," Abby had said. "There's no swimming here."

Holiday snorted. "I know that. I saw the checklist.

It's for the showers. You think I'm going to let anybody look at me naked?"

Holiday wore small white bras with scalloped edges, triangles against absent flesh. Abby wore undershirts.

Kiki looked at the map and agreed with Holiday. "This place is so dry."

Abby ran her nail over the topographical contours. "These maps are useless. On the ranch, we use township and range. That's what people really need to know."

Kiki put her palms on the table. "What's that?"

"It's what ranchers and oil people use. It's the best way to figure out where you are."

"Sounds really boring," said Holiday.

"Look, you gotta know your land if you want to ranch. Where the cows are going to be, where they might drill. You gotta know how much land you have, how many acres. Maps aren't for exploring or for helping you figure out where you're going. They're for telling you what's already there, right in your own backyard."

I opened the atlas on the table and turned to India. My fingers traced the country.

"I agree, they don't tell you where you're going. But I don't think they tell you what's already there either," I said. My hand ran over the seam of Pakistan. How many times would our family be split? Thatha's farm was too small for the map, but I pointed to Madras.

Amma had bought me Madras plaid shorts for camp. But the name meant too little to me. I could only conjure the bits I knew of Amma's childhood: the rosary beads, the roof, the sheets of embroidery, tutti fruttis, and the flagpole. Like names on a map, they gave me no sense of the whole.

Abby looked at the arrowhead of India on the page. An udder hanging off Asia.

"Maybe."

She told me that since she didn't have any brothers and sisters, the ranch would someday belong to her. She told me that recently her father had sat her down at their breakfast bar and laid a checkerboard map in front of her.

"'Learn this, Ab. You need to know that if anything happens to me, this—all of this—it's yours.'"

Poor Abby had looked at those black and white squares and thought that she might as well have been looking at a grid for a house plan—it didn't look like a map at all. But all those squares held her future. The rest of her life. She had a different kind of arranged life. Both of us girls in fates we couldn't control. Both of us shaped by a family history we had nothing to do with. Heirs to a place we did not choose to call home.

Our course began behind the lodge, near the dumpsters, which were shut tight with huge locks to keep bears out. Mrs. Watson had warned us about the dangers of keeping food in our tents on the first day of camp. I thought about my jar filled with curry powder, how it almost looked like the soil on the mountain— would a bear want that?

There was a red ribbon tied around a tree that marked our first waypoint. Abby read from Mrs. Watson's first clue. "'As you can see, you're at the beginning of a large trail. Follow it until it forks, then turn right. The path will immediately fork again, and you'll go right again and keep walking until you get to a sharp bend where you'll find the first red-and-white marker hanging.'"

We followed the path into the woods. When we got to the marker, we found another sign: "Follow the trail south to the junction and turn right, then onward to the next right and then a left. You'll notice the trail going slightly downhill, then slightly up again. This must be the small hill. If you look to the left, you'll see another marker."

The signs continued leading us along. There was very little growing on the forest floor beneath us, just pine needles crunching underfoot from the lodgepole pines looming tall and straight all around.

Holiday was at the back of our group. "They should make this camp coed. That'd be way more fun. We could get lost in the woods with boys!"

Abby focused on the map. I used the compass.

"I've kissed so many boys, I don't remember half their names," Holiday said. In truth, she had kissed exactly two boys. One was her cousin, and the other was her cousin's friend. It was during Thanksgiving dinner; they were all drunk off wine that they'd slipped from the table.

Abby didn't have time for boys. She missed too many days during calving season and went right home after school every day anyway—her bus ride was almost two hours long.

Kiki. She saw her mother's pregnant belly and hated the real estate agent. She would never marry.

And I had my uncle. Who needed boys? The girls saw my flat chest and skinny legs and knew I hadn't ever had a boyfriend. Which was true. And I wasn't going to tell them what I did know about kissing. So instead I told them about Amma's Harlequin romances. What I'd read about how kisses tasted sweet, how with a pinch a man could make your nipple hard.

Abby was clearly ready to move on. She led us to a dried-out creek bed. "I think this is the water we're supposed to be looking for?"

We all shrugged.

"It says to go downstream, and that we'll pass one boulder, then another that will be south of the stream-bed, and then a third boulder that will be in the stream."

She kicked the rock at her feet. It looked like a fat gray egg nesting in the bank. "'Turn east when you get to the largest boulder, then follow the trail so that you're once more going west.'" She put the map down and scanned the toothpick trees. Kiki sat on a rock.

"I think this is where we go, but I'm not sure," Abby said. "Does anyone else want to look at the map?" She held out the crumpled paper. Holiday took it.

"I'm, like, not sure this is really the boulder. We need to see three of them. I mean, this rock is big, but the others?" She gave the rock a kick for good measure.

"I'm pretty sure this is one of the boulders. There aren't a lot of rocks around here," Abby replied.

Kiki sighed. "If we get really lost, we're screwed. Does anybody even have any food?" All I'd packed for the day was a small backpack with a water bottle and my curry powder.

"We're not lost. The camp's less than half a mile away." Holiday laughed. "You think Watson tired herself out making this course? Does she look like she hikes?"

We all perched on the rock. A cracking sound rang through the trees, and two deer walked slowly down the streambed. One of them had a large rack that kept hitting the branches. They froze when they saw us, then Holiday pulled off her backpack and rifled for her camera. The deer turned and ran back the way they'd come.

Abby slid off the rock. "Come on, we need to get going or we'll miss dinner."

When we got up, I noticed a stain speckled the rock.

"Someone's bleeding," I said. I was a semi expert on this; AK Akka had explained a lot of things to me. And our copy of *Are You There, God? It's Me, Margaret.* was well-worn. Amma and Auntie Devi didn't wear tampons, but Amma bought them for Agatha Krishna. I saw the evidence of their bleeding every month though. The bathroom trash would be filled with bloody pads.

Each of us felt the back of our pants. Poor Kiki. We all turned to inspect her. There was a black stain soaking through her dark denim shorts.

"You're on the rag, man!" said Holiday. "You better watch it. Bears can smell blood. And they like it." Holiday took a picture of the rock with her camera.

Abby looked at Kiki. "I think we can walk back the way we came. It'll be shorter. We'll be back at camp pretty soon."

Kiki held her bottom. I dug through my backpack for a bandanna I'd bought at the outdoors store. Amma had told me to wear it around my neck. I gave it to Kiki.

Kiki took it and stuffed it down her shorts. "It doesn't normally happen this way. I'm just not that regular yet." Ever since her cat had been found in the tree, everything in her body had been off.

We walked back in silence. When we got to camp,

everyone was already at dinner and Sun was waiting for us on the porch, annoyed. She wanted to watch the World Cup, and we were keeping her from that.

"Could you guys have taken any longer? I thought we were going to have to send out search and rescue."

We mumbled apologies. In the lodge, Kiki made a beeline for the bathroom. She affixed a cheap pad with poor adhesive to her damp underwear. We filled our plates with salad and spaghetti. Cold, congealed garlic bread lay in baskets on the table.

Mrs. Watson gave us our orienteering badges even though we hadn't finished the course. And camp went on. We learned to square-dance. Holiday made friendship bracelets for every girl in the Alpine Forget-Me-Not group. Kiki read books and bled for eight days straight, causing her to miss her turn on the one horse at camp. I studied maps. I looked for clues of the kind of people who lived in certain towns. Were they near water? Mountains? A little valley? Why did they settle there? The world was so big, and Marley was just a speck.

I looked at Sacajawea's route. How did she make it all that way from her home? I was only about ten miles from Cottonwood Cross and entirely split between my desire to be home again and my relief to be away, tucked inside a canvas tent with a bunch of white people.

· · ·

And then, the end. The night of the pageant had arrived.

Mrs. Watson had invited all the blind campers from the Lions Camp down the road. They arrived and sat on crude benches made from lodgepole pines. Their white canes moved through the grass like antennae as they found their seats.

The sun set, and the mountain air cooled.

There was pine scaffolding on the stage to support the paper sets. Lights ran from the main lodge with extension cords.

"Well, another year has come and gone," said Mrs. Watson, to kick things off. "It's time now to circle the wagons." She wore a straw cowboy hat, a pink prairie skirt, and a white Western top with fringe. "We have a great show for you ahead, beginning with our Camp Sacajawea tradition, a reenactment of our namesake guiding Lewis and Clark to Oregon."

The audience clapped, and groups of girls in papier-mâché masks of antelope and moose, bear and coyote, pretended to graze on the stage. I wandered between them in a brown sack dress, a baby doll strapped to my back. My own short hair was slicked back with Dippity-Do.

I began my speech. About how much fun it was to guide these white men. How fun Lewis and Clark were!

Holiday and Kiki came onto the stage. They were dressed in suits. Abby had fastened ruffles down the front of Clark's shirt with crepe paper. Holiday wore a raccoon-tail hat and carried a big walking stick. They pretended to beg me for help. They needed my guidance. I played hard to get. The smaller girls onstage lolled their heads as if grazing on grass.

Finally I put the baby down in a basket and took Holiday's and Kiki's hands and began to lead them around the stage in circles.

"Look," said Holiday. "The ocean! Our redemption. See where Sacajawea is pointing." Kiki looked west.

Mrs. Watson began to play on a piano that had been rolled out into the meadow. The altitude and dry air made it impossible to tune, so the notes had a tinny aftertaste. A few girls began to sing.

Make new friends,
But keep the old,
For one is silver,
And the other gold.

The blind campers from Lions swayed to the music. Their white sticks tapped the earth, creating little clouds of dust. We began to sing in a round while the evening moths clotted under the lights.

"Crack your sticks!" Mrs. Watson called out. And one by one, we snapped our glow sticks so that waves of light lit the meadow. The opening notes of "If You're

Happy and You Know It" began. We sang and clapped our hands while Abby crouched by the side of the stage. She knew she would never see any of us again. Next summer, she'd be fourteen; there was no way that her father would be able to spare her from the summer work. But she was ready anyway; she was done with camp.

She clapped her hands. Holiday twirled the raccoon tail around her finger. Her glow stick stabbed through a buttonhole in her jacket. Kiki had taken her walking stick and leaned on it as if she was oh so very tired.

I kept still though. I didn't want to go home. I liked sleeping in the tent undisturbed. I liked using the bathroom in peace. I didn't like the chewy eggs and the bitter orange juice. But when I sniffed my curry, it also reminded me of the fog I felt around Cottonwood Cross. I wondered if, when Sacagawea got to Oregon, she'd felt relieved to have made it, or if she just worried about what these two men were going to make her do next.

I did want to go home though. To Agatha Krishna, whose breath, whose language, I knew as well as my own. To Narayan, who hadn't gotten to do anything at all that summer.

Sacagawea had been my age when she was kidnapped by another tribe, the Hidatsa. Kidnapped by other brown people. She was later sold to a trapper, and then forced into marriage at thirteen to that same trapper, who'd had another Shoshone wife named Otter Woman. Otter Woman would later disappear, but Sacagawea followed the trapper. He was the one who'd been asked to help Lewis and Clark. She was meant to be an interpreter. Like me—she told them the story they wanted to hear. William Clark called her Janey, presumably because her real name seemed too foreign to him. There is always a renaming. She hadn't wanted to go with them, but she did, and she saved their expedition several times as they continued west. She did what she had to do to get them all to safety.

When I got home, there would be two of us brown girls, finding our own way to safety. In the end, one would be lost. The other left to interpret it all.

A QUIZ:

IS HE BAD FOR YOU?

1. **Do you feel loved by your partner?**
   a. Yes
   b. No
   c. Sometimes

2. **Do you feel like you can have long, meaningful conversations with your partner?**
   a. Yes
   b. No
   c. Sometimes

3. **Do you feel like your partner listens to you?**
   a. Yes
   b. No
   c. Sometimes

4. **Do you feel like your partner cares about your feelings?**
   a. Yes, a lot
   b. No
   c. Maybe

5. **Do you think that your partner has always told you the truth about themselves?**
   a. Yes, definitely
   b. No
   c. You've had your doubts

6. **Do you feel like your partner is faking love just to have their way with you?**
   a. No, not at all
   b. Yes
   c. It's possible

7. **Does your partner use you for rent?**
   a. No
   b. Yes
   c. You don't know

8. **Does your partner feel bad when you're sad?**
   a. Yes, always
   b. No

c. You don't know, they have a hard time showing their feelings

ANSWERS

Mostly a: He's good for you! It seems like you two have a perfectly balanced relationship.

Mostly b: Run! This guy is bad news!

Mostly c: It sounds like you're a very passive party in this relationship. Stand up for yourself! Make sure your needs are being cared for! And if necessary, move on!

13

JULY

It was midsummer, and there was to be a royal wedding. Amma loved the Queen. Amma loved Diana. Amma sort of loved Fergie. But to be fair, Amma loved everything Anglo. And who doesn't love a princess?

When you think about it, the Queen is the ultimate Indian daughter.

Does what her parents say? Check.
Dresses modestly? Check.
Works hard? Check.
Duty? Check.
Arranged marriage? Not so much.
Love match? Check.

But the Queen is also the ultimate white woman.

Rich? Check.

Rich with inherited wealth? Check.

Her children get the best? Check.

Has nice designer clothes and jewelry? Check. Check.

Lives in a nice house? Check.

Colonizes other people? Check.

Doesn't think she's colonizing people? Check.

Is marrying rich winning?

Is marrying a white person winning? I wonder if Amma thought it was. Appa wasn't rich, and his skin looked like boiled shrimp after he'd been in the sun. Amma called him "Prawny." But she was glad his white skin had made us less dusky. And he hadn't asked Thatha for a dowry.

Amma knew her life was bigger. Bigger than Barnaby Road. Bigger than Kilpauk. Bigger than Madras. So how did it get so small? Working at a library? She was trained as a lawyer. She'd studied literature. She was meant for greatness. It's no wonder she leaves us with Vinny Uncle and goes out to work. It's the only life she has outside the house, the only means she has to carve out a space just for herself in the world.

Because no matter how accomplished she was, her future came down to marriage. It always comes down to marriage.

Amma didn't marry for a long time. She came back to India after England. She studied law. She started to practice. And then she decided to travel. To take one last trip before starting at a law firm in Madras. It was in England, when she was staying with Thatha's pen friend, Mr. Clay, that she met my father. A Texan on a post-Vietnam tour of England. They met in a pub in the Lake District. Amma was looking for daffodils. Appa recited Wordsworth to her. He followed her back to India, then she followed him back to Texas. Then to Wyoming.

Amma didn't know. She never knew. She might have killed her very own special brother if she had. Instead, she fought with Auntie Devi. They fought about how to cook idly. They fought about what channel to watch. How to wash saris and grease stains on pillows. They fought about whether we needed to wear coats. They fought over Vinny Uncle. They both brought him cups of tea. Auntie Devi's strong and dark. Amma's milky and sweet. Auntie Devi stayed in her room and watched soap operas all day long. When she arrived in Wyoming, she'd weighed less than one hundred pounds. Now she was all rolls. Narayan too was getting bigger and bigger. It was as if they were insulating themselves from Marley.

Sarah Ferguson got bigger after her marriage as well. Her Royal Highness the Duchess of York only saw Prince Andrew forty days that first year they were married. He was always off somewhere in his helicopter. She was always alone in the palace.

Appa too left Amma to plant daffodils. He was off on rigs eating tinned fish and crackers. He was away at the man camps while Amma named Cottonwood Cross, while Amma made a home for us. What other model did she have? Sarah Ferguson was a princess, and even she had to obey.

How could someone be the ultimate white woman and the ultimate Indian daughter all at once?

Diana was the only one who showed us something different. Diana never obeyed. We'd never seen anything like it. Diana and Charles's wedding was the first thing we ever taped, and Amma watched it over and over again on our Betamax.

But that summer, watching Sarah Ferguson arrive to Westminster in the Glass Coach, we knew she was no Diana. We knew she would never do anything to compromise her fairy-tale ending.

We all want a happily ever after.

But maybe happily ever after is the most dangerous thing you can have.

July brought the royal wedding, and it brought the country fair and the rodeo too. And while I wouldn't arrive to either in a glass coach, I had my own rules to obey.

I entered sewing and the Fashion Revue and the cake-decorating competition.

I had to make a dress for the Fashion Revue. I had to model it on the runway. And I had to decorate a cake.

How a person presents herself/himself through clothing, grooming, facial expressions, and body movement is a form of communication. Have you ever thought about what your clothes say about YOU?

The goal of Fashion Revue is to develop an understanding of personal presentation in public situations with regard to clothing, accessories, and grooming.

I'd read all about how the Queen sends out secret messages with her clothes. She wore a dress with poppies on it when she visited California because poppies are the state flower. Her wedding dress was embroidered with spring flowers to show Britain that renewal was possible after the war. She fidgets with her handbag whenever she wants to get out of a conversation.

My dress for the revue was made from a sari. Everyone else in the Silver Spurs had gone to the fabric store, but Amma had said no. That oil was down and we needed to use what was at home. Her saris were nicer than anything you could get at JoAnn anyway, she said. I just couldn't cut any sari with gold on it. Or the one with the hand-dyed circles.

I chose a pink cotton fabric with small, embroidered birds. Agatha Krishna had chosen a sari with birds on it for herself when she got her period.

My dress was nothing special, just a tea dress with buttons up the front. The buttons were the hardest part.

When you're on the runway modeling your dress, everyone's watching you. You have to walk a certain way and watch how you swing your arms. You have to sit in a chair on the stage and hold yourself perfectly still. The instructions are exacting:

You must hold yourself in T position.

Half turn—Begin with your feet in a "T" position, lift heels slightly, pivot in the direction of the back foot. Pause. Pivot back to the original position. Toes never leave the floor. By sliding the forward foot behind the other foot, you may reverse the position of the "T." By turning halfway and walking from there, you can also change the direction of movement.

This is what being a girl is like. Holding yourself in a specific position, only moving when someone tells you to.

I won a blue ribbon. But I didn't go on to the state fair. Only the champions go on for that. Blue isn't enough. Blue is just enough to say *you tried*. Blue is just enough to say you are a duchess and not a princess.

. . .

Sarah Ferguson and Prince Andrew had two cakes at their wedding. Two rum-soaked marzipan cakes almost six feet tall. They had two made in case one got damaged.

For the fair, I just had to make one cake. Yellow cake. It was a piece of cake! Even with the adjustments for altitude.

Amma said that I had to tell a story with my cake. That's how you win. And so, I decorated my cake with roses. I told the story of Thatha and his roses in Kerala. Everyone likes a grandparent story.

I won Reserve Champion.

I did the cakewalk alone. It was to raise money for 4-H. There was a whole row of cakes. Buttercream. Fondant. Cakes shaped like teddy bears. Cakes shaped like cats. American flags. Clovers. Butterflies out of icing perched on the frosting.

A jaunty polka.

Full step, half step, half step.

Full step, half step, half step.

The music stopped.

You don't know where you'll end up when the music stops. Life's always like that.

I was standing on the number eight. The MC called out my number. I won. I chose my cake.

Cake for everyone that night as we watched the tape

of Charles and Diana again. And then of Andrew and Sarah. We watched them do their perfect dances. We watched everyone wish them a happily ever after.

I have never said aloud what Amma didn't believe— that happiness came from dumb luck. It comes from standing on the right square at the right time. It has nothing to do with work. Amma believed in the fairy tale. Maybe she had to. Maybe that's what kept her going. Diana's unhappiness, Sarah's unhappiness, they were not unlike her own. Marriage was not what she thought it would be. Marriage was sitting alone at home, waiting for your prince to come back. It was following the rules that had been set forth for you, no matter what.

I didn't want any of it.

Which is why the cake wasn't the only thing I mixed that month. Well, actually—it was Agatha Krishna who mixed spoonfuls of Prestone into Vinny Uncle's sodas. She didn't make any adjustments for altitude. She knew I was only good at following a recipe. She knew I studied the rules and followed them. And she wanted him dead by the time school started. She wanted to have her cake and eat it too.

14

YOU

Look, I know you've been patient. You love crime—
I do too. My podcast queue says it all: *Betrayal, Over
Someone's Dead Body, The Cold Case.* And so on.

But I know that what you really like is white crime.
It's less interesting if it's a brown girl who's dead. Even
less if it's a brown man.

Sure, you like our bodies—you always have. Our
bodies plucked tea. Cut cane. Picked cotton. Were your
ayahs. Soldiers. Drivers. Sweepers. Cleaned up all the
messes you left behind.

Even now, brown bodies work for you. Tidy your
hotel rooms, your house, care for your lawn, make your
fries.

No? Not you? Okay, what about yoga? That's how
you think of our bodies, right? Twisted and pliant.
When people ask me if I do yoga, when they look to me

in a class, I move to child's pose. Lying on the ground. Head bent. Knees bent. I'm not a threat.

"You're not very flexible," teachers say.

And I think, *I have bent so much in my life, I can't move anymore. I am so accommodating I can barely breathe.*

But now I rise into mountain pose, facing you. Now I'm ready to impose, to tell you what happened. Is it more interesting when the brown girl kills? Is it interesting when she says, *This is enough?*

It is an acknowledged truth that to be a girl is to be extracted. Girls, we are taken.

For once, we were the ones who were going to extract. We wanted to be the ones to take. To take Vinny Uncle right off the earth. Right out of Cottonwood Cross. Right out of the family. Right out of our bed. We were going to extract his life, so precious to him, we knew, but without him, our own lives would be worth so much more.

A QUIZ:

DO YOU HAVE WHAT IT TAKES TO KILL?

1. **Do you want to be independent?**
   a. Yes
   b. No

2. **Do you want to put the two halves of your divided self back together?**
   a. Yes
   b. No

3. **Do you want to rid yourself of the shadow that seems always to be following you?**
   a. Yes
   b. No

4. **Do you want to stop feeling so *split, split, split*?**
   a. Yes
   b. No

ANSWERS

Mostly a: It must be done. You are Kali. You have a garland of skulls and stand on men. Feel her rage and wild eyes.

Mostly b: You are not Sita. You mustn't walk around asking people to believe you. That you are pure. Save yourself. She is not the one to look to.

15

AUGUST

Amma said we were pioneers, not so different from the ones who'd traveled the Oregon Trail. She pointed to a trunk she kept in the garage and told us that she'd come to the US of A with no luggage but that. She'd tell us the story of coming to America with that one trunk, how she was the first Indian in Marley—our kind of Indian, that is. Marley was already home to the Apsáalooke (Crow), Tséstho'e (Cheyenne), Očhéthi Šakówiŋ (Sioux), and the hinono'eino' biito'owu' (Arapaho).

Amma reminded us of the hardships she'd faced, how when she'd come, she'd traveled carrying X-rays of her chest in her hand to prove that she didn't have TB. She told us these stories whenever we complained about Marley. About Wyoming. How we hated the wind, how there was no amusement park. She told us we were lucky to have beds, heat, a full refrigerator. And I guess we were.

But do you know what pioneers do?

They colonize. They take things that aren't theirs.

A pioneer is a person who claims they are the *first to go*. Claims they are the *first to explore*. *First to settle*.

Like Kit Carson. Like Lieutenant Marley. Like Lewis and Clark.

We had to become pioneers if we were going to kill him. We had to do what was best for us, no matter how it might affect other people. That's what pioneers do. That's what colonizers do.

Many years later, Fort Marley would finally acknowledge that the founding of the town came at a dire cost to Native nations and peoples.

The Wyoming history book that I grew up with tells this story of Marley. That Lieutenant Marley was a hero who protected telegraph lines and the citizens of the Dakota Territory. He made a fort. Gathered some white men. And the Indians attacked him. Strikes on Fort Marley increased after the Sand Creek Massacre. (Was it sixty-nine or six hundred Indians who died there?) How do we tell the story of this place? In plaques? Every summer the Battle of Fort Marley is reenacted by local men. They put on tanner and shoe polish to play the Indians. But the perception of the story shifts with time. A Wyoming history book now would say that Lieutenant Marley wasn't here first after all. And he wasn't that much of a hero. Actually, he'd hurt many, many people.

You have to acknowledge wrongdoing, or it will never heal. Vinny Uncle never acknowledged it. He was just like Lieutenant Marley, doing whatever he liked, regardless of the cost to others. Who was going to rewrite our story? Who was going to say what he did to us was wrong? He wasn't. So we had to.

There was a reason that as I got older, I started watching crime shows almost exclusively. Those people got their day in court. They got to have a jury of their peers say *You were wronged*. We would never have that. Vinny Uncle would never say sorry. He would only ever say *Don't tell*. He would only ever say how much he loved us.

But AK Akka told me that history was on our side. That time would tell that Vinny Uncle hurt us, that he hurt other people too. That even if we got caught, eventually people would see the truth.

I was like a poor civil servant, I told myself. I was just following the law. That's what Amma would say about so many Indians under British rule—they were just trying to live their lives, didn't want to make waves. That was me. And the law was AK Akka. I was doing what I was ordered, so no matter what happened, it couldn't really be my fault. She had become so very British. So very much like Lieutenant Marley. Or was she Gandhi? She told me she was trying to make us free. But all I could think was, we weren't being very nonviolent at all.

We killed him on August 14. One day before the anniversary of India's independence. Thirty-nine years to the day since Thomas Ayyar said he was *felîca* in Esperanto. Thirty-nine years to the day since my mother had sung the "Jana Gana Mana."

When you're colonized, it's like the words in your throat are dissolving like a cough drop, disappearing into an imposed mask of sweetness that keeps the noise your body's yearning to make from coming out.

Killing my uncle was like screaming. And we had to scream. At the end of the day, we knew that no acknowledgment, no apology, no rewriting of our history could ever change how we felt. We didn't want a sorry. We wanted it to stop.

Let me tell you this:

The way my mother tells it, Jesse Owens taught her to run. I had never heard of Jesse Owens before she told me that. "He won the Olympics," she said. He was Black, Amma told me, and had come to India, to Doveton Corrie, and taught a group of girls, all in white dresses and white Bata tennis shoes with soles like paper, how to run. It was 1955, eight years after India became independent. "He told us to keep our bodies low and our arms swinging," she said.

The next time we played tag, I ran as she advised. I looked a bit like a penguin, wings flapping, never taking flight. Sonata caught me with ease.

Jesse Owens won four gold medals in the 1936 Berlin Olympics and in doing so, proved that Hitler was wrong—Aryans didn't have athletic supremacy. After the Olympics, Owens came back to a segregated America and struggled to make a living. He worked as a sports promoter, in a dry-cleaning business, and as a gas station attendant. For a period of time, he made money by racing against horses. There are grainy You-Tube videos of him running around a field, a horse with a jockey bobbing on its back trailing behind him.

Even when he first came back to America, not long after he landed, there was a ticker-tape parade in his honor in New York City, followed by a reception at the Waldorf Astoria, but he had to take the freight elevator to it. He was a man who knew about being split.

Keep your body low and your arms swinging.

We had to discipline ourselves. We had to give Vinny Uncle the drink. We'd bought antifreeze at the Mini-Mart and hid it with the 3-IN-ONE oil and gasoline for the lawn mower. We had no idea how much to give him, or how long it would take. We started small and then began to *pour, pour, pour.* When the drink was mixed, he didn't seem to notice. He smoked all day, and I am sure anything tasted sweet on his tongue.

In the end, it took almost three weeks.

Even for us, a white person dying was more interesting. On the day my uncle died, one other person in the state of Wyoming was also killed. Her name was Lilith Jones.

The circumstances of their deaths were incredibly different.

Vinod Ayyar died at 1:20 in the morning following a brief illness, while Lilith Jones died after a tragic accident in which she was hit by an oncoming car at 3:14 in the afternoon.

Vinny Uncle died shortly after arriving at the hospital. He had been vomiting and feeling ill on and off for two weeks.

Lilith Jones was killed on the side of US Highway 287. She had stopped her car to look at a herd of antelope. Ms. Jones was not from Wyoming but from Michigan. She was visiting relatives in Glenrock and decided to take minor roads rather than I-25 from Denver. Antelope were new to her. She had seen deer galore,

but "antelope were a creature of God she had not wit-
nessed," the newspaper wrote the next day, quoting a
cousin of hers from Louisville, Kentucky. She pulled
her Honda CRX over to the side of the road and got
out to look. Later, the driver of the truck that hit her
would state she was not at the side of the road or even
near her vehicle. He would state that she was in the
middle of the road. "Like a prairie dog," she stood still,
fixed as he approached. He came upon her soon after a
curve in the road, and he admits he was flipping a tape
in the tape deck. He hit her at fifty-five miles an hour.
Her body flew onto the shoulder—and on the prairie,
the antelope ran in a loping gait toward a nearby snow
fence. The driver, a sixty-seven-year-old man named
Darren Carpenter, cried on the news as he recounted
the story. He hadn't seen her until it was too late. He
was so sorry.

Agatha Krishna and I were partial to the story of
Lilith Jones. For one thing, her death was far more
spectacular than that of Vinod Ayyar. His death was
mentioned only in the obituaries of the local paper, and
as per Aunt Devi's request, no autopsy was done. The
death of my uncle, who drank heavily and smoked more
than a pack a day, was not seen as a suspicious death.
Although he was young, he'd lived hard, especially
since he'd moved to America. In the weeks leading up
to his death, he had gone to a KISS concert and had

partied at the county fair. He had a weak heart. Rheumatic fever as a child.

Our hearts. They were becoming blacker.

We were done playing tag. Done freezing.

It was time for him to *freeze, freeze, freeze*.

16

SEPTEMBER

Hey! Be aggressive!
B-E aggressive
B-E A-G-G-R-E-S-S-I-V-E
Be aggressive!

I heard Agatha Krishna practicing her cheers and I knew that's what we had done. We'd been *aggressive, aggressive, aggressive.*

When he went to the hospital, Agatha Krishna put the antifreeze bottle in her backpack, walked to Washington Park, and threw it away. We never talked about it again. Agatha Krishna didn't talk to me at all unless it was necessary after that.

"You don't need to worry anymore. He's not coming back," she said, to justify separating our beds, to explain why she'd started going to bed after me, after her long skin-care routine; the room would already be dark by the time she came in.

Our great-grandfather's pen pal, Mr. Clay, had plans to come visit us that month with his wife. The timing was bad. But they were going to Canada for Expo '86 and then planned to come south to Marley. He'd been our great-grandfather's pen friend for nearly thirty-five years, and although Thomas Thatha had never met him, they had exchanged many letters, in both Esperanto and English. Mr. Clay had sent him rose seeds and once even a bottle of 4711 cologne and a bar of Yardley's English lavender soap. When Thomas Thatha finally died, a cousin doused his body in 4711 as it lay on a charpoy in the house.

We hadn't put 4711 on Vinny Uncle when he died in August. I didn't even see his body. He died at the hospital, having been rushed there in an ambulance. He'd been vomiting, his speech slurring. He'd left a glass of lemon-lime Gatorade on the nightstand. Agatha Krishna washed it out, handwashed the glass, and then placed it in the dishwasher. I was glad she had done the pouring and the washing. I thought we would be happy, but instead I felt dread. All I could think about was whether Auntie Devi would order an autopsy.

But Auntie Devi just continued to work. We all

thought she would stay home in mourning, but the Monday after the funeral, she put on her smocked apron and name tag and asked my mother to drop her at Gibson's. Appa had come off the rig to take care of the funeral arrangements. Amma sat in the back garden drinking sherry.

Narayan stopped playing video games and instead lay in bed reading Archies. He drank the leftover Mountain Dew and wrote letters to his paati in Madras. But when school started a week later, Narayan didn't miss a day. None of us did.

It wasn't as if we weren't sad. It was sad to see Vinny Uncle's work boots by the door. His ashtray on the deck. But we hadn't known what else to do.

A week later, Vinny Uncle was back home, in a black lacquer box that Auntie Devi put on a dresser in the bedroom. As soon as she and Narayan were able to travel back to India, his ashes would be put in the family cemetery, with some kept out to scatter in the Indian Ocean. But there was no money for tickets now. Oil prices were still *down, down, down,* and Auntie Devi's savings from Gibson's wasn't enough for her to travel even to Denver.

The Clays' coming was a welcome break from the stillness that had settled on Cottonwood Cross. Appa was back on the rig, so Amma gave them her room. She washed the sheets and placed marigolds in a small vase on the nightstand by their bed, along with a pitcher of water and glasses.

Appa did come home again at the end of the month to give the Clays the full Wyoming tour. They had it all mapped out. Jackson Hole. Yellowstone. Across the top of the state to Devils Tower, then over to South Dakota to see Mount Rushmore. England may have cathedrals and theater and London, but it didn't have a rock with the faces of four dead men carved into it.

Amma stocked up on Lipton tea for the Clays, plus Smucker's marmalade and a big tin of Danish butter cookies.

When they arrived, they gave me and Agatha Krishna Portmeirion mugs, and for Amma, they had good English tea (which they would drink all of in the ten days they stayed with us) and a bag of shortbread that had been smashed to crumbs in transit. For Narayan, bars of Cadbury chocolate and Percy Pigs, and for Auntie Devi, a bar not of Yardley's but Imperial Leather. Which perhaps had really been intended for Vinny Uncle.

The Clays drank endless cups of tea, starting with breakfast, which for them was just two slices of toast each. In the afternoon, they drank still more tea, accompanied by three butter cookies apiece. They talked endlessly about their daughters. They were good girls.

Their daughter Beryl worked in finance in London, and their other daughter, Rosemary, had three children and stayed at home. We'd heard about them from Thatha, who knew more about the comings and goings of the Clay children than he did of us. It annoyed Amma that when he called, he would tell us all about them. As if he had a better family in England.

We ate out a lot while the Clays were staying with us. Mr. Clay said he liked a good curry, but neither Amma nor Auntie Devi cooked for them. Instead, we had burgers on the grill and took them to the Sizzler for steaks. They went to Denny's and ate breakfast for dinner, which delighted them. Mr. Clay said they had excellent Indian food in England. He liked chicken tikka masala, a dish I had never had. But he had an ulcer and was trying to stick to bland foods. I think Amma was happy not to have to cook for them. Auntie Devi too.

It was during their visit that I read a long article about anorexia in AK Akka's *Seventeen*. The next morning, I decided to see if I was capable of not eating. I drank cups of tea without milk like the Clays did and divided up one butter cookie to nibble on.

I lasted one day that way. I was too hungry.

After that I stole some of Narayan's chocolate and *ate, ate, ate* from the butter cookie tin. I filled up on yogurt and crackers and cereal. My stomach puffed out like a ball. I smoothed my uniform shirt over it and wondered if I looked pregnant.

I tried to throw it all up. I stuck two fingers down my throat, but my body stopped them from going too far. A kind of defense mechanism. I took my toothbrush and tried again. Nothing. And then I remembered my babysitting kit. I had taken a babysitting course at the YMCA earlier that summer, and they had advised us to make a kit to carry with us at all times when we baby-sat. Mine had a pad of paper and a box of crayons, some Band-Aids, a first aid kit, a deck of cards, an old coloring book, a copy of Enid Blyton's fairy tales, and a bottle of ipecac.

I administered a spoonful of ipecac to myself in the bathroom, then waited. Nothing seemed to be happening, so I wandered out to where the Clays and Amma were drinking tea.

"Want a cuppa?" said Mr. Clay.

"No," I said. "I'm just feeling a little off."

Amma felt my head. We had a thermometer, but she never used it. She had her own remedies for any ailment: rasam for a cold, clove oil for a toothache, a warm washcloth for almost anything else, unless you had a fever, in which case the cloth would be cold.

I went to our room and lay down on my sleeping bag on my bed, which I'd been sleeping in ever since I got back from camp. I liked zipping myself up tight.

I felt my stomach flicker and ran to the bathroom.

Up came the Cadbury Fruit & Nut chocolate bar.

Up came the butter cookies.

Up came the Honey Smacks.

Up came the Yoplait.

Up came the Tang.

I thought of Vinny Uncle. How he had thrown up in this same toilet. He must have wondered what he ate. I hated to think I was like him. Curled over. Sweating, his stomach buckling, seizing. I wondered if he lay on the bath mat looking up at the ceiling, seeing the same view we had seen for months.

But I knew what was wrong with me; he'd had no idea.

I wiped my mouth and lay on the tiles, not wanting to go back into the room I shared with Agatha Krishna. It felt so small now. I felt her eyes on me. And her silence.

I breathed in and out and tried to speak in Angel's heavenly language.

I'm sorry.

I'm sorry.

I'm sorry.

All that came out were apologies.

The morning after he died, when Amma and Auntie Devi came home crying, we were all in our places.

Narayan on the pullout couch in the living room. Agatha Krishna and me in our beds. Our father in a trailer in the Powder River Basin, checking the depth and operation of a well. Agatha Krishna heard the car in the driveway and went out. I could hear her talking with Amma. She was gone for only a few minutes, then came back to our room. She unzipped my sleeping bag.

"It's over. He's gone." She grabbed my forearm tightly. "I took care of it. The glass. The bottle. And now we can never speak of this again. Ever." Her nails made little moons in my flesh. "It's all good. Keeliti." She pulled me up into a hug. So tight. "We will never ever speak of this. Swear on my head." She didn't give me time to answer.

I scrambled out of her embrace.

"Never, I swear."

Father Duffy had told us not to swear on anything.

"If you do, I'll die. Swear on my head."

"I swear on your head." I touched her short hair that was stiff with hair spray. I didn't want Agatha Krishna ever to die.

She rolled out of my bed and crossed the crack to her own.

When I think back to that morning, I remember the light outside the window was a warm yellow. I could hear chickadees and robins and the tick of the Moores' sprinkler. Angel's aunt always watered as the sun rose. She saturated the ground before it got too hot.

I shouldn't have sworn to do anything. Especially not on Agatha Krishna's life. But that promise, made early in the morning, was one I would stick to. I would hold fast to it like a life raft and never say a word. I don't think Agatha Krishna ever told anyone either.

I thought with him dead that we'd be able to *breathe, breathe, breathe.* But instead, whenever we saw each other, we were reminded of what we had done. That we had watched him watch a pay-per-view boxing match on HBO and refilled his glass and not felt even one iota bad. We had brought him a poisoned cup while everyone else sat on the deck playing Monopoly. We'd left it for him, grabbed a handful of chips, and not thought anything of it.

His death exposed us for what we were: sinners. We'd broken the sixth commandment. And the fifth. And honestly, the tenth, as we had coveted a life that didn't have late-night visits or trips to the bathroom.

But were we really sinners if all we wanted was to be safe?

We had been aggressive and we never spoke of it. But we also didn't speak at all. Our speech became the pleasantries of roommates. Agatha Krishna never got into my bed. She never talked to me about boys or school or anything. I wasn't sure if we had won or lost. Our secret language was gone.

Amma did her best while the Clays were with us to entertain them, to engage them in conversation. Mostly because she knew that Thatha would call and ask. She asked if they'd seen Charles and Diana while they were in Canada. Amma knew they'd gone to Expo '86 as well. The royals had opened it, so the Clays had not, in fact, seen them. Mrs. Clay—Mary—had seen the Queen when she toured the Lake District in 1956 though.

The US theme in the expo was space, but no one mentioned the *Challenger.* No one mentioned Vinny Uncle either. None of the dead or dying. Mr. Clay did note that the USSR pavilion was all about nuclear power—and wasn't that a pip! With Chernobyl having happened just a week before the fair had opened.

"You never know when disaster will strike," Auntie Devi said, nodding into her tea. She was still wearing her name tag from work, which read, *Deb.*

"Oh, yes, horrible business, Chernobyl," said Mrs. Clay.

Amma cupped her mug. Bits of sugar spilled onto the table. Her hands were shaking. To her, her brother's dying was worse than any nuclear disaster.

The Clays' visit went on forever. Agatha Krishna missed most of it because she'd become a cheerleader. She had practice in the evening every day.

I listened at night through our door while she went through the routines. She'd pushed our two beds apart and practiced her splits between them.

We say: Go!
You say: Fight!
Go! Fight!
Go! Fight!
We say: WIN!
YOU SAY: TONIGHT!
WIN . . . TONIGHT!
WIN . . . TONIGHT!

Her pom-poms rattled, and I knew she was looking at herself in the mirror. Her Saints cheer uniform on. Later, before a game, she and the other cheerleaders would paint stripes on their faces like war paint. These girls, these Catholic girls, chanting:

Hey! Be aggressive!
B-E aggressive
B-E A-G-G-R-E-S-S-I-V-E
Be aggressive!

They would go on to have children in their teens, stay in Marley and work at the mall, or maybe in an insurance office.

Only Agatha Krishna would leave town. Only Agatha Krishna would fight her way out of Marley's grasp. She would leave us all. She would leave me. A year from now, we would have our own rooms again. A year from now, the only time I'd feel that Vinny Uncle was near was when I went to the bathroom, when the overhead light flickered and the water was on, drowning out all the other sounds.

A QUIZ:

HOW DO YOU DEAL WITH
A BROKEN HEART?

1. **What's the first thing you do when you're heart-broken?**
   a. Seek support from your loved ones. [*Unless it's your loved one who broke your heart.*]
   b. Privately reflect on the relationship and your feelings about it. [*Yuckaduck.*]
   c. Avoid thinking about it entirely. Do everything you can to distract yourself. [*Go to school. The mall. Work on your sticker book: Stick the Sandylion bears all in a row.*]

2. **How do you cope with overwhelming sadness after a split?**
   a. Allow yourself to feel and express your feelings. [*Cry, cry, cry, but always in the bathroom so one knows.*]
   b. Nurture yourself. Have a spa day! [*Steam your face.*

Make a mask of egg yolks. Spray yourself with Jean Naté.]

c. Smother your feelings and stay busy to avoid the pain. [Quiet, quiet, quiet, *but stick your finger in Fun Dip and taste the sour. Swallow it down.*]

3. **How do you tend to feel about your love life after a breakup?**
   a. Positive and open to new opportunities. [*Ask Angel if she would like to be blood sisters.*]
   b. Circumspect but hopeful for better experiences. [*Pray to St. Blaise.*]
   c. Pessimistic, doubting the prospect of love. [*Write in the diary with the key, "I will never have love."*]

4. **How open are you to forgiveness after a relationship is over?**
   a. Believe in forgiving for your own peace of mind. [*We are truly sorry and humbly repent.*]
   b. Open to forgiveness but take time to process. [*We no longer push the beds together.*]
   c. Hold on to anger. [*She made me do it.*]

5. **Do you reach out to your ex-partner after a breakup?**
   a. Rarely, unless necessary for closure. [*Pardon me, do you have any Grey Poupon?*]

b. Occasionally, for closure or to check in. [*Whatchu talkin' 'bout, Willis?*]

c. Regularly, hoping to restore the relationship. [*How do you spell* relief?]

6. **How important is it for you to seek professional help or therapy?**

a. Open to therapy as a resource. [*We do not believe in therapy.*]

b. Will consider therapy if needed. [*We do not believe in talking to strangers.*]

c. Cowboy up! [*We do not believe in medicine. Amma uses clove oil for a toothache.*]

7. **In the long run, how do you envision your emotional recovery after a broken heart?**

a. Believe in healing and growing stronger. [*Like Lazarus.*]

b. Expect gradual improvement as time passes. [*Like the Cold War.*]

c. Fear that you may never heal. [*Like nuclear war.*]

ANSWERS

Mostly a: You're going to be okay!

Mostly b: It will take time!

Mostly c: The road ahead is long.

17

OCTOBER

There was a way I was taught to tell a story. Mrs. Feeney, my fifth-grade teacher, drew a crisp triangle on the board. Next to it, she wrote three words: *CHARACTER, SETTING, PLOT.* Then she drew a stick figure and said our stories needed to have a *who* that the story happened to. Underneath the figure, she wrote *Jane.* There also needed to be a *what* that Jane wanted; she asked us all what we thought Jane wanted. Hands shot up across the room. Heather said to date Mike, the cutest boy in school. Mike said a new Barbie. Narayan said chocolate. Mrs. Feeney took Narayan's answer and wrote *Jane wants chocolate.* And then she said we needed to ask *why* Jane couldn't have chocolate. Did she have a strict mother? Was she allergic? Was the Mini-Mart all out? She said our story would be set in Marley and that Jane's quest for chocolate would be the plot.

"Now it's up to you! You must determine the *conflict*

of the story! Does Jane get her chocolate? If so, *how* does Jane do it?"

She said the story would resolve itself when Jane either got the chocolate or gave up, and that either way, a lesson would be learned.

And that is how I learned to tell a story.

A ghost story is a different kind of story though. In a ghost story, the who could be a ghost that appears by magic, or because it's inextricably drawn to a place. But the who could also be someone who is haunted by a ghost. Someone who has unfinished business with the dead.

I didn't dare talk to Mrs. Feeney about that, didn't dare ask her who the who would be in a demon story, as she called them. She was sure Satan was around every bend. She told us stories about horrible people who she said would sacrifice our dogs and cats on Marley Mountain. She claimed she'd seen a pentagram made of rocks in a field near the Bi-Rite. She told us heavy metal was the devil's music. She told us to keep an eye on our cats. Poor Pops could have been killed by satanists.

None of that scared me though. I already lived in a haunted house. And everywhere I turned that October, there were more ghosts.

Angel made two ghosts out of a volleyball and her brother's basketball. She draped white pillowcases over them and cinched their necks with yarn and drew their eyes on with markers. She draped them from the cottonwood that bordered our two houses. Every time we pulled into the driveway, the specters waved in the wind.

Seeing them, I wondered about Vinny Uncle's soul, wondered if he would come back to haunt us. I wondered if he knew it was us who killed him.

Meanwhile, we were still trying to decide what to be for Halloween. There was no money for anything from the store, but we were good at repurposing things in our house. I wanted to be a gypsy, so I wore a long hand-blocked skirt of Amma's and piled on bangles and costume jewelry and wrapped a silk scarf around my head. Narayan wore a gorilla mask that Auntie Devi had brought home from Gibson's and his normal clothes. Someone had returned the mask because the eyes weren't level with each other. Auntie Devi took her sewing scissors and tried to even them out, but you could still see Narayan's thick glasses through the holes.

Agatha Krishna put on her old confirmation dress and poured talcum powder on her head, took Amma's kajal and made thick rings around her eyes. She dressed as a ghost, though she didn't need to; she already was one. Her weight was dropping. She didn't see Jason Parks anymore. She stared off into space. And once, I found a bottle of Vinny Uncle's Jack Daniel's in our closet.

When Agatha Krishna went to a sleepover, I went with her. I'm not sure why—maybe Amma wanted time to herself without us. It wasn't until I was older that I realized how hard it must have been with Appa always gone. In that way, she must have been happy when Vinny Uncle came to live with us, even if the phrase *live with us* was never uttered when we spoke of them moving in. They were always just going to stay until they could afford a place of their own. But Vinny Uncle's work paid very little, and the job at Gibson's only gave Auntie Devi what Angel's mom called mad money—or as Angel's aunt Barb said, pin money. Aunt Barb warned all us girls to have pin money. She used hers to buy Crown Royal, and gave us the purple sacks to keep our treasures in.

Amma never asked the parents of Agatha Krishna's friends if I could spend the night too. She just dropped us both off and left before the family had time to give me back. I wasn't invited to many sleepovers myself, though Angel slept over plenty. Agatha Krishna had never seemed to mind when I came along before, but after what happened, she did. Everything about me seemed to make her unhappy then. She told me I was grody. Grody to the max. I, in turn, said this to Narayan.

"You!" I said, poking his rounded belly. "You are so grody! Grody to the max!"

Narayan's eyes were rimmed red, and a single tear

came out. He went outside and climbed a tree. I did not go to him.

Who had I become? I was cruel. But when I saw him, there were moments I saw Vinny Uncle. The same bright white teeth and skin. The same haircut. Narayan would smile, and I would see him. I didn't want to do a thumb war or arm wrestle. I didn't want to touch him. So he sat and played Atari and barely talked to anyone.

But Agatha Krishna's friend Mindy Lacey had a little sister two years younger than me, so I guess that was why Amma felt she could deposit me at their house with AK Akka for a Halloween sleepover. Mindy rolled her eyes when she saw me.

"She'll tell!" she said.

"No, she won't." Agatha Krishna may not have liked me anymore, but she knew I wasn't a snitch.

Mindy Lacey lived with her mom and sister, Kathleen, in a small ranch house near ours. Her street was called Rendezvous Lane. Her mother smoked, and the whole house had a stale, cold smell. Her mother opened the windows, but it did nothing to air the place out.

I really wasn't a snitch. I hadn't told anyone about our babysitter who watched the Playboy channel. Or that Agatha Krishna stole candy from the Mini-Mart. Or that she'd dated Jason Parks. I hadn't told anyone when she and Angel mixed a bag of frozen strawberries and Crown Royal in the blender to make daiquiris. I'd said nothing when she pocketed the small white lipstick samples Auntie Devi had been hoarding from the Avon lady, who'd been stopping by with great regularity these past few months. With Vinny Uncle gone, Auntie Devi had taken to wearing heavy perfume. And more makeup day by day. Amma told her blue eye shadow made her look like a tart. At first I'd thought the lipsticks were tiny tampons, but they had their names stamped on the bottom: Blue Flame. Ripe Cherry. Honey Bisque. Copper Penny.

Of course, the biggest reason that Agatha Krishna knew that I wasn't a snitch: I had told no one about our uncle.

Now Mindy looked at me solemnly. Her sister, Kathleen, was asleep on the couch. Her mother was out on a date and would come home later, smelling of Lady Stetson and nicotine.

"We're going to conjure the dead," Mindy said, and headed to her room. "We're going to lift the veil and help the unsettled spirits get to the underworld!"

We followed her. She pulled out a thin board game from under her bed.

"It's a Ouija board. My dad got it for me."

Agatha Krishna looked at me. "We're going to have a séance."

"Maybe we can talk to your uncle!" Mindy said.

I did not like this at all. This was devil stuff. I also

knew that Vinny Uncle was not in heaven. But he had been murdered, so maybe not in hell either. His soul, I was sure, was in purgatory. A place that Mrs. Lynch, my old teacher, told me was worse than hell. A place where unsettled souls wandered and tried to settle their unfinished business on earth. I wanted no part of it. But I was with Agatha Krishna, and I didn't want her any madder at me. I didn't want them to think I was like Kathleen.

Mindy set up the board, took out one of her mother's cigarettes, and lit it.

"You're supposed to cleanse the energy in the room." She waved it around, then brought it to her mouth, inhaling deeply. She put it out in a glass of water on her desk and took our hands to make a circle around the board. Her room was covered in posters of two Michaels. Jackson and J. Fox. She had a pink canopy with a ruffled bed skirt. My dream bed.

"We call upon the spirit world, come talk to us." She closed her eyes and looked deep in concentration. She placed her fingers on the planchette and Agatha Krishna laid her index and middle finger on top. I didn't like the eye on the board. It was watching us.

Between the cigarette and the low lighting, my head hurt. Mindy with her eyes still closed began to hum. It reminded me of Angel when she fell into a trance.

I didn't want to mess with Satan and the under-world—I wasn't sure whether Satan was the devil or my uncle. But I placed my fingers on the planchette any-way. The room reeked of smoke, and I could feel my heart beating in my chest. I could hear the TV from the living room, lulling Kathleen to sleep. The laugh track every few seconds punctuating the silence.

Nothing happened.

"We call upon the spirit world!" Mindy repeated. "Come talk to us!" I felt the planchette slowly move across the board.

"Can you hear us?" Mindy whispered.

The planchette moved to *YES*.

"Did you live in this house?"

NO.

"What's your name?" The board stopped, then slow-ly started to spell out letters.

Z-E-B-R-A

"Zebra!" She pronounced it *Zeb-ra*. It didn't occur to any of us that *zebra* was the name of the striped ani-mal. Or that there was a pack of Fruit Stripe on Mindy's desk. In that moment, Zebra sounded like the name of some exotic woman.

"Are you a good spirit or a bad spirit?"

The board stilled. The smoke reminded me of Vinny Uncle. I began to feel lightheaded. The laughing from the living room turned into music. I could hear a synthesizer but couldn't make out the words.

And then Mindy's bedroom door opened with a

whoosh. We all screamed. Kathleen stood in the doorway, the hem of her nightgown tucked into her underwear.

"I am so going to tell Mom." Then she sat down to join the circle.

After that night, Agatha Krishna seemed hell-bent on calling up the dead. Amma would never have let a Ouija board come into the house, so Agatha Krishna would gather us up to play Bloody Mary instead. She lit one of Amma's oil lamps or a candle and told me to take it into the bathroom. Narayan would hang back. Our bathroom had no window, so when the door was closed, no light could get in. It was the perfect room to play in. Agatha Krishna had told me to hold the lamp in front of my face, look in the mirror, and repeat "Bloody Mary" three times.

Bloody Mary
Bloody Mary
Bloody Mary

My face looked shadowed in the mirror. I studied my reflection. Did I see a monster? Or was she behind me?

Or was that just myself?

Mr. Clay had written a long thank-you note earlier that month, with two updates on life in London. One, that the M25 ring road that looped around the city was almost finished, and two, that a new show had opened on the West End called *The Phantom of the Opera*. It was a play about a ghost who lives under the stage at an opera house. One of Mr. Clay's former students played one of the lead roles. He told us how the boy had been a chorister and that he'd always thought the kid had what it took to go far. He cut out a review from the *Times* with the headline "God's Gift to Musical Theatre," which I knew Mrs. Feeney would find scandalous. There was a photo of the phantom, his half-masked face leering at me.

I looked at my own face in the mirror again. There was no doubt—I knew that the true monster was me.

I left the bathroom and handed the candle to Narayan.

"What did you see?" he asked.

"Just me. Just my reflection," I said, not making eye contact with AK Akka.

"I want to talk to Appa," he said, his face dark in the shadows.

"No, no—this is just to see Bloody Mary," I told him.

"Appa."

In the half-light, I could see the tears on his cheeks.

"Father Stewart told me that God needed him." His voice rose. "But I need him." He began to cry in loud sobs. "What's going to happen to us without him?"

In the candlelight his face looked like the picture of

the phantom too. I wiped his tears with the end of my sleeve. Agatha Krishna stayed quiet. We hadn't much thought of Narayan when we'd bought the antifreeze from the Mini-Mart.

"Nothing is going to happen," I said. "Your appa is in heaven, waiting for you. But he's telling you not to hurry! You're going to stay here with us for a long time. Nothing's going to happen to you."

We were not a hugging family, but I stroked his arm. AK Akka sighed and walked to our room. Wax ran down the side of the candle onto the carpet.

"Mrs. Feeney says some people get stuck between heaven and hell. That's where ghosts are."

"He's not in between," I lied.

But then I thought about the time Narayan, Agatha Krishna, Angel, Sonata, and I were playing in Amma's car in the driveway. We were pretending to drive to Denver. Agatha Krishna put the car in reverse. We slowly started to roll down the driveway. We rolled into the street. Amma, Auntie Devi, and Vinny Uncle came out of the house. We were all crying. Angel and Sonata ran next door, and Amma comforted us—nothing had happened, we were okay. AK Akka sheepishly gave her the keys and promised never to play in the car again. But Vinny Uncle looked at Narayan and removed his belt. He took Narayan back into the house, and we knew he was in trouble. Even though he hadn't even been driving. AK Akka looked away, but I watched as Vinny Uncle marched Narayan inside.

I wanted to tell him that we had saved him too.

He wiped his face and let out a breath.

"I'm going to talk to him." He stepped inside the bathroom, shutting the door.

I was already in hell.

Come Halloween we stumbled around the neighborhood, knocking on doors and trick-or-treating. Narayan loved Halloween and filled his pumpkin buckets with chocolate and suckers. He still couldn't believe all you had to do to get candy was knock on a door. Angel, Sonata, and Bison came with us, and after making our rounds, we all went back to Cottonwood Cross to compare our hauls.

Agatha Krishna hadn't gone trick-or-treating with us. She had stayed home and given out candy instead. Her talcumed hair gave off a sweet smell, and her blackened eyes made her look like a raccoon.

Once the rest of us were half drunk on chocolate, she told us to go up to the room that she and I shared.

The oil lamp flickered on our dresser.

"I need you all to make me levitate," she commanded. She didn't make eye contact with any of us.

Angel snorted. "You want us to do devil things!" She put her hands together and began to speak her heavenly language. "Om, chevroletta, nutmega, Oh, windy woo . . ." She rattled off her nonsense words.

Agatha Krishna ignored her.

"Maybe it's an angel that will lift me up."

Angel stopped gibbering and knelt next to AK Akka, who had lain down on the carpet, talcum powder making a halo around her head.

"You all need to put two fingers under me." We put our hands on her.

"Repeat after me. She's looking pale. (*She's looking pale.*) / She's looking worse. (*She's looking worse.*) / She's dying. (*She's dying.*) / She's dead. (*She's dead.*) / Light as a feather, stiff as a board. (*Light as a feather, stiff as a board.*)"

We repeated the last lines again and again. *Light as a feather, stiff as a board.* Agatha Krishna was fading away. I could see it. I could feel her ribs underneath my two fingers. I pressed into her flesh. Into her soft side. I had curled into her night after night for years like a cobra. Now we slept as if there were a moat between us. The dresser between our beds a kind of closed-up drawbridge.

I wasn't sure why she didn't want to be here. We had done what she wanted. And now it seemed like she wanted to join him.

But no matter what we did, she would not lift. I wondered if it was her soul that was lifting, looking down on us as we chanted. I had felt my soul go out of me in the bathroom, with Vinny Uncle. But it always came back. With Agatha Krishna, though—she did not come back. I felt her soaring away like a phantom.

Years later, I learned that the Phantom of the Opera was not a ghost at all but rather a disfigured man living under the stage. A man so shunned by the world that he lived alone, hidden beneath the rhythms of life.

To be a ghost is to be a dead person who manifests themselves for the living. Vinny Uncle was not going to appear. And like him, Agatha Krishna was disappearing.

And disappearing was all she wanted to think about that fall. Disappearing from me. From Amma and Appa. From Marley. She channeled her frenzy to leave into whatever outlet she could, but the one that made me most uneasy of all was MASH.

At the beginning of the game, someone would write the word *MASH* across the top of a piece of paper, and from each letter, going vertically down the page underneath, they'd write the following words:

Mansion   Apartment   Shack   House

Then you came up with a bunch of categories, and underneath each category you listed four options for your future. Agatha Krishna loved making the catego-

MASH

Marry ♡
Michael Jackson
Father Duffy
Mike Jhonson
Crocodile Dundee

Job
Model
Mom
Doctor
teacher

How many Kids
10
5
3
none

Where you'll live ☆
Marley
New york
Paris
L.A.

Car
TransAm
Limousine
Beetle
Bike

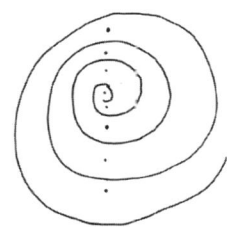

ries and was constantly changing them out. Who were you going to marry (Michael Jackson, Father Duffy, Crocodile Dundee, or Mike Johnson—the cutest boy in eighth grade)? Your job (teacher, doctor, model, mom)? How many kids would you have (ten, five, three, none)? Where would you live (New York, LA,

Paris, Marley)? What kind of car would you drive (Trans Am, bike, limo, Beetle)? What pet would you have (cat, dog, gerbil, pig)? Money ($1,000,000, $10,000, $1,000, $0)?

Let's say it was Agatha Krishna's turn to have her fortune told. Angel would draw a swirl on a piece of paper, spiraling outward until Agatha Krishna told her to stop. Then she'd draw a line through the swirl and count how many times the line intersected with it. Maybe there'd be seven; she'd begin to count from the top, from the *M*, seven words through the categories, crossing out every word she landed on until each category had only one option left—Agatha Krishna's future.

Agatha Krishna would watch as Angel went, hoping all the while that she wouldn't end up a mom with ten kids, married to our priest, living in a shack in Marley. She wanted out. And she made it. Days after high school, she was gone; she never looked back. The mountains we grew up with meant nothing to her. I think she told people about being from Wyoming as a kind of party trick. Marley was just a funny place she was from. I also tried to leave, but I always came back. The choke of trees and buildings and people were not for me. I was fated for the high plains of Marley.

The triangle. The ring road. The halos. The spiral on the page. They're all ways of creating order. But the center would not hold. I was so tired of spirals and twists. We lived in the West. The road was supposed to be straight and clear, only horizon ahead, with not a turn in sight.

I didn't need a game to tell me my future. It was to stay in Marley, haunted. Agatha Krishna was the ghost rattling around inside me. She could not live there and could not leave. And so instead she knocked over lamps, chilled the rooms, stopped talking to me. I hadn't done anything wrong, and now she blamed me. She didn't need to go to the bathroom to remember. I reminded her of all the bad things that had happened every time she looked at me. We were connected forever, whether we wanted to be or not.

What I was realizing was that what Mrs. Feeney had taught me about how to tell a story wasn't quite right. In life, there isn't always a resolution. What did I want? My sister. Why? Because that's what a sister is—part of you. The only person who knows that monsters don't come from the closet, they come through the bedroom door.

How do I get her back? I had no idea. But every day there was less of her. Her shadow was bigger than an india-rubber ball. It was all around her, circling her like a ghost.

18

YOU

I take it back, what I told you in the beginning. This story isn't for you. It's for her. For my sister, who slipped out of my hands that year. I've told you that my uncle split us in half. He split us in half twice. The first time he split us apart from ourselves. The second, he split us apart from each other. He was still hurting us, even after he was tucked away in his box on the dresser.

Maybe you have a sister. Maybe you have a brother. Maybe you have both. So maybe this all makes at least a little bit of sense to you. I had thought everything we'd been through, what we'd done, would bring us closer. Instead, after all of it, we couldn't even look at each other.

I can say it to you. If I had known I would lose AK Akka as well, I would not have killed him. When people do you wrong, they live in your skin every day. You brush your teeth, you think of them. You go to sleep, you think of them. Years later, your child will jump into your arms and you will react by pushing her away, not wanting to feel anyone coming at you that fast.

I had my tonsils removed when I was eight. Years before the Ayyars came. I packed a little suitcase and got new pajamas, and Amma told me I could eat ice lollies and pudding for every meal. Agatha Krishna came to visit me the day I was in the hospital. She brought me a little present, a sign with a unicorn on it. It read, "Discover the magic within yourself." She thought I had magic in me then. She sat on my bed, and we cried at being apart for a night. We were bosom sisters, which was so much more than being bosom friends.

Perhaps we would have grown apart as adults regardless. Maybe she would have moved to a big city and left me in Marley. Or she would have married Jason Parks and had all the babies in Marley. Or she would have married Mindy Lacey and lived in a house with a garden. Or become a doctor and served in war-torn countries. Or died in an accident.

There are a million ways to live.

I want the words to tell you I am sorry. Not for what he did but for never talking about it. For letting him take her further away from me. If I'd talked about it, maybe he would have had to stop. Maybe they would have moved out. Moved on. Agatha Krishna and I would talk about it as that terrible time that Amma's family lived with us. The one time that Vinny Uncle touched us and Amma said stop. But none of that happened. Instead, we danced around it, used words that didn't exist to tell each other it was bad.

Your sister is someone who shares your blood, has the same currents coursing under her skin.

We thought that would be enough.

You know this.

In this, we are the same.

19

NOVEMBER

Amma always used to tell us a story about a flowering tree. Her grandmother, her paati, had told her the story, and every year in Kottarakkara, the story would be told again and again, by aunties and cousins. Amma says there's a recording of Paati telling the story somewhere, that some white people came and spent a day recording all her stories and eating her green mango fish curry. She has no idea, though, where that recording went or how anyone would ever be able to listen to it.

But in the story, Amma said, a poor girl turns herself into a flowering tree. It takes two pots of water to turn her into a tree, and two pots of water to turn her back into a human. When she's a tree, her sisters gather her flowers and then transform her into a human again. They weave the flowers into garlands and sell them at the market. After that, they are no longer poor.

But one day, a prince sees the girl, falls in love with her at first sight, and marries her. She can't believe her good fortune. But her new sister-in-law does not like her, does not think her worthy. She makes her perform her trick for her friends. So the girl turns herself into a tree, but after she does, the sister-in-law and her friends rip off her branches, tear out all her flowers, and then abandon her; they don't help her turn back into a human. She gets wet in the gutter, and then the girl is left a human carcass—nothing more than a torso—to wander the streets. I am not sure how a torso wanders. But that's what Amma said. The prince could not find her.

I can't remember how he eventually recognizes the torso as his wife, but somehow he does, and he pours two pots of water on her and then she is beautiful again. They go home, and the sister-in-law is put into a barrel of burning lime. The tree girl holds no anger for anyone though. Even as a tree, she had accepted her lot in life.

It was a woman's fate to stay quiet and hope everything worked out. In all the stories Amma would tell us, the girls never rose up. They accepted their fate, they married. They were dutiful and obeyed.

They never killed a man.

That story is often considered to be an environmental one. A lesson in conservation. The tree girl must be treated gently; you're only supposed to pick the flowers, nothing more.

But someone always wants more. Someone always takes too much.

For us, though, it was a story about family, how family can turn on you. Agatha Krishna and I thought the prince was daft for not seeing the bad seeds in his family. Though by that logic, Appa and Amma were daft too.

We'd joke about our own flowering trees—maybe it was best to make a joke. Agatha Krishna had been getting her period for almost a year, but my tree had not flowered. Each month she dramatically took a box of pads into the bathroom.

"I have to go deal with my flowering tree," she'd say.

Once, years earlier, we'd decided to become blood sisters in our bathroom. Agatha Krishna took a razor blade and made a quick cut on one of her fingers, then another on one of mine. We rubbed the wounds together.

"But aren't we already blood sisters?" I asked.

"Yes," she said. "But now I'm choosing you as my sister always. Not just because you already are."

It was logic that made little sense to me. I knew we had the same blood. But I took it the way I took most things then, not with logic but with acceptance. I believed what most anyone told me.

What I couldn't say is that I wanted even more of her blood inside me now. I wanted that bit of how she swung her pom-poms and curled her hair. The way she wrote her scripts and banged her pestle. Amma said we had the same blood, but I wanted more of hers. I wanted her sureness as she measured the first dose of antifreeze into one of the little medicine cups that came with our liquid Tylenol. For her, everything about Vinny Uncle was black-and-white, while for me, it was a bit gray. She had believed that killing him was the only way for it to stop forever. That even the pain of his death would not hurt Amma as much as the truth. But I had almost told her. When she cut our hair for lice, I had almost told her that her brother was a parasite. But then she told a funny story about Kottarakkara, about a summer when all the cousins had to have their heads shaved, and I couldn't ruin what little she had left of India.

We saw two movies that month, both on the same weekend. *Song of the South* and *An American Tail*. My teacher Mrs. King had told me we would like *An American Tail*. "It's about immigrants," she whispered. "Like you." I didn't have the heart to tell her that Agatha Krishna and I were not immigrants. We'd been born right here in Marley.

Auntie Devi took us to see both movies. Appa was

home for the weekend, and Amma wanted us out, so Auntie Devi deposited us at *Song of the South* and mall-walked while we zip-a-dee-doo-dahed into the theater.

Song of the South is the only movie that Disney keeps in its vault. The only movie they will never show again. They never released it on video at all. But in 2041 it will be in public domain.

First made in 1946, they rereleased it in 1986 for its fortieth anniversary. People didn't think it was quite as racist then. It's set in Georgia and based on old American folktales. I bet someone from Disney sat with an old Black woman in Georgia and made her tell them Uncle Remus stories into a microphone. I wonder if she ever knew what happened to them.

Uncle Remus is the star of *Song of the South*, alongside his friends Br'er Bear, Br'er Fox, and Br'er Rabbit. Uncle Remus was nothing like Vinny Uncle or any uncle I knew. He told stories like no other. Stories about his animal friends and stories about the Tar Baby. The Tar Baby wasn't a real baby, but rather a doll covered in turpentine and tar. Poor Narayan—that movie was so popular that year, he got called Tar Baby at school for months. He was the darkest of us all, and like the Tar Baby, he never said anything. He'd swing by himself on the playground at recess or twist the tetherball around its pole.

In the movie, a rich white boy named Johnny goes

on vacation to his grandparents' plantation. He tries to run away, but instead meets Uncle Remus, who tells him stories. He entertains him because it's *boring, boring, boring* to be left at your racist grandparents' plantation. Uncle Remus tells Johnny African American folktales and then he makes friends with a Black boy named Toby and (as Heather Ross put it at school) a white-trash girl named Ginny.

Johnny wouldn't have lasted a month in Marley. We would have hanged him from the cottonwoods. He was always whining; was even attacked by a bull. And all the while, the brown folk helped him. But Johnny was white and rich, so no matter what happened to him, he knew he'd be fine. He wouldn't grow up and marry a poor girl from the wrong side of the tracks like Ginny or have brown friends like Toby for more than the summer. He would remember Uncle Remus from his fancy club in Atlanta, remember that time in his childhood when he'd lived on a plantation.

For boys like Johnny, sunshine would always come their way. It was their birthright.

But we were flowering trees, waiting for someone to cut our branches.

Amma told us that folktales were never written down. They lived by being told, and as such, they were always transforming. We spoke our own version of them, to suit our circumstances. For us, for instance, the girl always transformed into a cottonwood or a crabapple—we'd never seen a jacaranda or flame of the forest.

Br'er Rabbit was my favorite part of *Song of the South*. I had always liked rabbits. I had a stuffed jackalope, another folktale. And Vinny Uncle had a piece of paper taped up on the wall beside his bed that read, "SAY RABBIT." He'd told us that the first words out of your mouth on the first day of the month needed to be "Rabbit rabbit." If you said that first, you'd have good luck for the whole month. He kept the paper there just to help him remember. It was still there on the wall, two months after his luck had run out.

Their bedroom had very little in it. A crucifix on the wall, which still had Agatha Krishna's wallpaper; there were dried palm fronds tucked behind Jesus's knees. Propped up on the dresser was a picture of my dead paati and of Thatha, in his dhoti and blazer. I never saw any photos of anyone in Auntie Devi's family. I knew she wasn't from Madras, but from somewhere near the tip of India. Near Tirunelveli. She was a rural girl.

Eventually, she remarried a white man and moved to Denver. When she was widowed again, she donned white clothes and a crucifix and moved back toward Tirunelveli. She built a house and had a servant there who rubbed her feet and oiled her hair. Who made her fish fries and listened to her stories of America. She spent her time painting, and occasionally sent pieces back to us in Marley. Amma had a stack of her paintings, all of orchids and coconut trees. She never hung any of them. By that time, she didn't want to remember. By that time, she was looking forward. To the marriages and babies we weren't giving her. To the months with seemingly no luck in sight.

20

YOU AND YOU,

or

A QUIZ:

HOW EASY IS IT FOR YOU/ YOU TO FORGIVE?

1. **When something's gone wrong, or someone has done you wrong, do you:**
   a. Turn the other cheek! This is about them, not you.
   b. Time for revenge. But maybe not murder.
   c. Do nothing, but spend all your time thinking about doing something.

2. **Do you keep your distance from the person who caused you pain?**
   a. Yes. Time and space heal. You wait for them to connect and talk.

b. Yes. Why be around someone who caused you pain? Close the door on them.

c. You weren't involved. The roots of the wound started long ago. You can only make reparations.

3. **Do you find it's hard to rebuild trust after something has gone wrong in a relationship?**
   a. Yes. You are wary of letting new people in.
   b. No. Their loss! You'll just find new friends.
   c. Why do you trust everyone? Don't get involved with anyone who's done you wrong!

4. **Do you find it difficult to be nice to those who have harmed you?**
   a. Yes and no. You like to think that maybe they just made a mistake.
   b. Nope. What they did was inexcusable.
   c. You weren't involved. They were mad about something else and took it out on you!

5. **What is the benefit of forgiveness?**
   a. Anger is not a place where you can live.
   b. Nothing. The satisfaction of cutting people off feels better.
   c. You weren't involved. But you can apologize for those who came before. You can make reparations.

6. Do you think amends can be made and reconciliation can heal?

    a. Yes. If it's in a safe space.

    b. No.

    c. Acknowledgment is the first step. Isn't acknowledgment enough?

7. How does memory affect forgiveness?

    a. If you can forget, it's easier to forgive.

    b. If you can't forget, it's harder to forgive.

    c. You have no memory. It was before your time.

ANSWERS

Mostly a: You're a kind person but perhaps also naive. Don't be a doormat! Let your kind nature lead the way, but make sure to take care of yourself too.

Mostly b: You have to let go of your anger. Don't forget what happened, but try to embrace forgiveness too.

Mostly c: You easily forgive. But also too easily let yourself off the hook. Think about volunteering! Or some sort of service to ease your guilt! You must make the past right.

21

DECEMBER

A.

It was December, and it was cold. Narayan was Joseph in the school pageant again. I had been demoted. We had a new student named Jasmine Garcia, and she was Mary now, so I was just an angel.

We got our tree from the lot outside Gibson's that year, and made ornaments out of salt dough. We stuck cloves in oranges. We chewed on the cloves for as long as we could stand it before sticking them into the peel. Amma gave us cinnamon sticks too, to eat as candy. We gnawed on anything that filled our mouths with spice.

I'm not sure what Agatha Krishna said to Amma or Appa to explain our beds now being wide apart. But her Christmas gift that year was a waterbed. It was full-size, so it took up more than half the room. We could never put our beds together again.

Agatha Krishna took that bed very seriously. Once a month she'd take the broom and carefully roll the handle down the mattress, moving all the air bubbles to the spout and then slowly letting them out. The bed would make a little burp. She had only one set of sheets for it—waterbed sheets were expensive—and she washed them herself. She tended that new bed as she never had her previous. It was the only safe place for her.

Sometimes I'd get into her bed when she was at cheerleading practice. She kept the heat up high, so it was always warm. I rocked my body until the bed made small waves.

Merrily merrily merrily merrily . . .

Life is but a dream.

Agatha Krishna would smooth all the imperfections out of the bed. The bubbles that made it noisy and uncomfortable. The bed was fixable.

On New Year's Eve we stayed up till midnight. We said "Rabbit rabbit" when we woke up the next day. We would do anything for better luck. We would do anything to fix what we had done.

B.

It was December, and it was cold. Amma was again standing on the heat register. She had lost weight since

Vinny Uncle had died. Her nightgown hung on her but poofed above the vent. She was like a little bell on that vent, like a Victorian lady in a big hooped skirt.

"Tintinnabulation! Tintinnabulation!" I would shout.

Amma used to tell us words she loved and that was one of them. She also liked *mellifluous* and *supine.* She was often supine in those days. I wanted her to be happy again. I also wanted to shake her side to side like a clapper to bring some life into the house. Everything had gotten so quiet.

Only Auntie Devi moved with purpose. December was a busy month at the store, and she had signed up for extra shifts. She brought home all sorts of things that month: candy canes, broken ornaments, a nativity set that was missing the baby Jesus.

It was while I was hunting for hidden Christmas presents with Narayan that I found the bottle in her room. Narayan wanted Construx and a G.I. Joe Cobra Terror Drome. I wanted Pound Puppies and some Jean Naté—Agatha Krishna said once you turn twelve, you start to stink down there.

Auntie Devi and Narayan kept their suitcases in a row in the closet, waiting for the day that they'd either move to another house or go back to India. There had been talk about them going back ever since Vinny Uncle had died. Amma thought they should go home, where Auntie Devi could have servants and Narayan would be with other cousins, Auntie Devi's family. But Auntie Devi dug in. She did not want to be a widow there. And her trump card was always that Vinny Uncle had wanted Narayan to be raised in the US of A.

Their suitcases were all hard sides, except for one small, plaid soft side with a front pocket. Narayan was looking under the bed when I felt something hard through the fabric of the suitcase.

I unzipped the pocket and pulled out a bottle of antifreeze.

At first, I thought she'd found our bottle. That she was keeping it there, waiting to get us. Biding her time until just the right moment to bring it out and ruin us. But ours had been a yellow bottle, and this one was blue. And anyway, I knew that AK Akka had thrown ours away in the park.

There were some papers in the pocket with the bottle. I scanned through them, saw the words *ethylene glycol*, a series of numbers. It looked like homework.

"Did you find anything?" Narayan asked. "There's nothing under here except this."

He held up a bag filled with underwear and a silk nightgown. Lingerie. Underwear with lace and bows. The nightgown was nothing like the kinds that Amma or Auntie Devi normally wore, which were long and shapeless, high to the neck with sleeves.

"No, nothing here." I wanted out of the room. I shoved the papers back into the suitcase.

Narayan held a bra by his pointer and thumb. "Do you think these are for Auntie Indira?"

"Amma? No!"

You could see he wanted them to be for anyone but his mother. His widowed mother who, in India, would have had to wear white and shave her head because his paati believed in the old ways. His paati wouldn't have even wanted Auntie Devi to eat a jalebi.

"She got these on sale; they're for no one! They were just a good deal!"

Narayan held the bra like a dosa. He was so easy to fool.

I waited until that night to tell Agatha Krishna. Her back was to me in her waterbed. Her bed undulated a bit as she tossed and turned. I knew she was awake. I knew her breathing better than my own. I lay on my back and looked at our ceiling.

"We didn't kill him."

She was silent. But I knew she wasn't asleep. The bed moved slightly.

"What are you talking about?" she finally said. "He's dead."

"I know, but we didn't do it," I said. I couldn't help it—for some reason, I started to laugh.

"What's wrong with you? He's in a box on the dresser. We did that." Her voice raised in pitch, almost bordering on shrill.

"But we didn't." I stopped laughing. And then I began to cry.

We had started poisoning him in July. We hadn't known how much, so we'd just put in a spoonful or so. We knew if we put in too much, he wouldn't drink it. But he favored sweet drinks, pineapple soda, Mountain Dew. We hadn't ever increased the dosage much as it always seemed to make him vomit a lot.

"I found a bottle of antifreeze in Auntie Devi's room. In her suitcase. It was almost empty."

Agatha Krishna was silent. She turned toward me and sat up. Her body convulsed in waves, and I wasn't sure if she was shaking or if it was just her bed.

"And there were notes, with math and numbers." I needed her to understand. "Don't you get it? She's a scientist. She knows what to do. All we did was make him sick. We didn't know how to kill him."

I'm not sure what was hitting Agatha Krishna in that moment. That we had failed to kill him. That we didn't need to feel guilty anymore. Or that Auntie Devi was a killer.

"Is the bottle still there?" she asked, swinging her legs over the side of her bed. "Did you take it?" Her voice was steady.

"Narayan was in the room when I found it," I said. "We were looking for presents. So I left it."

I had thought that Agatha Krishna might come to me. Hold me so I could coil against her. But instead, she started to cry. I stayed on my side of the room while she cried and cried. In the morning, her eyes were still red. But I never saw her cry again after that. Nor did either of us comfort the other.

Two days later, when Auntie Devi was at work and Narayan was at nativity practice, I took AK Akka to the room and showed her the bottle. She held it in her hands, and then asked me to get her backpack. I brought it to her and she put the bottle inside, told me she was going to the park to get rid of it. She took the papers too. It was a sunny day, but cold. She put on jogging pants underneath her cheerleading skirt and pulled on a pair of Amma's boots.

While I waited for her to return, I put everything back the way we'd found it. I noticed that the closet was full of new clothes. Auntie Devi was spending her pin money on a new version of herself. One of the suitcases in the closet was filled with saris, and there were matching sets and sweaters in every color of the rainbow on the hangers. She also had a curling iron. She'd always borrowed Agatha Krishna's before, but on the dresser, next to Vinny Uncle, was a brand-new one.

When Agatha Krishna returned, she had a ripped

piece of one of the papers in her hand. She went back into the bedroom and put it on Auntie Devi's dresser. We left.

She wanted Auntie Devi to know we knew. That we'd taken care of it.

I'm not sure how long Auntie Devi had known. Both what Vinny Uncle had been doing and that we were trying to kill him. Narayan moved around. Sometimes he slept in bed with her. Sometimes on the pullout couch. When we were in the tent, in one of our beds. Vinny Uncle worked nights. In the day, she was gone, and he slept. When we came home from school, if Amma was out, he would mix us Tang and give us an apple. Narayan would go to his Atari and we'd be alone with him. Auntie Devi and Vinny Uncle only really crossed paths for a few hours in the early evening once she got home from work.

I didn't know much about marriage then. My own father was barely home. I didn't think Amma was unhappy, but she spent her days out of the house. And when Appa would come home, she would cook big meals and then they'd lock themselves in their bedroom.

Auntie Devi and Vinny Uncle seemed separate from each other though. I barely saw them together, and at dinner, when we were all around the table, she kept her head down, looking at her hand as it scooped up rice.

I always felt bad that Amma never did anything with Auntie Devi's paintings. Always coconut trees and orchids. Flowers and trees. Amma would say after they moved out a year later, after Narayan had gotten into Stanford, that maybe Auntie Devi wasn't as simple a village girl as she'd thought. Agatha Krishna and I never said anything in return. How could we tell Amma how much Auntie Devi was worth? How could we tell her that simple village girl had saved us?

C.

It was December, and it was hot.

I think you want to know if we were okay. If Agatha Krishna and I ever found our footing again. Whether we killed him or not.

I have told the story to you. And now I am spiraling again. I think back to Lilith Jones. The woman whose death we thought was more important. Or at least more interesting. I think about that day, when Vinny Uncle vomited and vomited and then went into a coma. When the ethylene glycol snaked through his body. From us? From Auntie Devi?

That day, looking at the antelope, Lilith Jones left her body. For a moment, she was double. She was seeing something wild, something so primitive and outside herself that she didn't feel the smack of the car, didn't feel herself get dragged away.

I wonder if it was the same for Vinny Uncle. He was split too. Split in his marriage, in coming to America, in being a little brother again, in working in the night, in calling himself Vinny rather than Vinod. I wonder if he saw light or lingered above his body as he slipped away.

Isn't it something that I can look back at him with some tenderness?

In high school, Angel got into drugs and was arrested for shoplifting. She was living with her aunt again, going to the Wyoming Behavioral Center for court-ordered therapy. She told me that place was worse than hell. But she told me something else that I'll never forget. Something her therapist had said to her. "'Angel, you can have a good life in spite of your mom, or a bad life because of her.'" She dragged on a cigarette after she told me that and said, "I guess I have a bad life because of her."

I lost track of Angel. I don't know if she had a bad life. I look for her every few years, and in my mind, I have made a story of her life. I always picture her with children, teaching them her heavenly language. Teaching them to say *Do not be afraid* again and again in her own tongue.

A good life in spite of. In spite of bad ancestors. In spite of your skin. In spite of colonialism. In spite of capitalism. In spite of nationalism. In spite of the internet. In spite of war. In spite of the patriarchy. In spite of lists of things you want. In spite of a man who came in the dark and did things that he shouldn't. *In spite. In spite.*

On my one trip to India, Agatha Krishna and I took Amma's ashes to Kanyakumari. Amma always said it was the place where three waters meet. The Bay of Bengal, the Arabian Sea, and the Indian Ocean. A land's end. It was an auspicious place, a place you could never *chop, chop, chop.* A place where things flowed together.

Kanya Kumari was Lord Krishna's sister, so this is a place of sisters too. Amma called it Cape Comorin, the British name, a distorted version of Kumari. Some people know only the new name, only the Indian one— they weren't there for the split. They've known only the after.

Kanya Kumari was so full of rage at being stood up by Shiva on their wedding day that she destroyed their wedding feast. The small stones on the beach are thought to be grains of rice from the wedding that never was. Then a demon king, Banasura, tried to marry her, but she killed him—she was so full of rage at being wronged. She wouldn't let herself be taken. As Banasura died, he repented and asked for forgiveness.

It is said that in those waters, you can still be absolved of your sins.

And so Agatha Krishna and I waded in. Amma moved further and further away from us as we swam. So did Cottonwood Cross. And the daffodils and cottonwoods. And the glasses of Tang and Pops the cat. And the suitcases and that bathroom. I held the plastic bag in my fist and dipped myself under the water. Above me was blur and brown. I felt Agatha Krishna try to pull me up. Her hand was underneath my armpit. But instead of coming up, I pulled her into the warm water with me. I grabbed her hand and tugged her under.

In Tamil, when we leave we say, நான் போடிற்று வாறேன்—*Naan poyitu vaarein.* "I'll go and come back." I will go and come back. Agatha Krishna had always told me that she'd go, and she had. But now I was once again moving my body into hers. Now we once again held each other. I didn't feel half anything. It was the closest I'd felt in so long to being whole.

It was a marvel. In spite of it all, she had come back.

ACKNOWLEDGMENTS

Katherine Fausset, my agent. First reader. First believer.

Naomi Gibbs, I am so very thankful for your laser instincts, deep discernment, kindness, and wisdom. You have made me a better writer. I am so grateful to have worked on this book with you.

To my exceptional team at Pantheon, who have guided my book with vision and immense thought: Lisa Kwan, Michiko Clark, Bianca Ducasse, Juliane Pautrot, and Lisa D'Agostino. For bringing my book to life: Linda Huang and Joan Wong.

Bill Thomas and Denise Oswald, for publishing peculiar books and not being afraid to do so.

Special thanks to Beth Lamb and Barbara Richards, for handling all my work with such care.

For their art and imagination, Romano Nickerson and Abby Gibbs. And to Dr. Whitney Cox for checking my Tamil.

Acknowledgments

And to Lisa Lucas, for taking a chance on me.

To the Homewood Suites, Residence Inn, and Candlewood Suites. Hotels that I made into mini residencies. The waffle machines and quiet got me through.

I have benefited from the help of many institutions. Huge thanks to:

My colleagues and the English Department at Colorado State University. Especially Ramona Ausubel and Andrew Altschul. And a special thank-you to Emily Daley for being my compass.

The University of Wyoming Honors College and Peter Parolin, Caroline McCracken-Flesher, Susan Aronstein, and Donal Skinner.

The National Endowment for the Arts, for supporting writers and literature and being my fairy godmother.

Huge appreciation to the Wyoming Institute for Humanities Research, for a semester of work and mentorship.

To the Wyoming Arts Council and Michael Lange, particularly, for supporting art across Wyoming.

The Radcliffe Institute for Advanced Study at Harvard University gave me time, space, and a community of scholars who shaped this book. I especially thank the Walter Jackson Bate fellowship. Ayodele Casel, you inspire me to no end.

To Jennifer Sahn and the team at *High Country News* for regularly helping me reimagine the West.

Thanks to the City of Fort Collins, Colorado, for my Art to Live Grant.

Acknowledgments

To my community at Fishtrap, a place that reminds me why I love words. Gratitude to Shannon McNerney and Mike Midlo.

I am immensely grateful for the love, guidance, and friendship from Laura van den Berg, Steph Opitz, Antonya Nelson, Leah Schlachter, Surabhi Balachander, Vauhini Vara, Laura Pritchett, Katie Freeman, Meena Venkataramanan, Elena Passarello, Caroline Casey, Tanaïs, Molly Messick, Mira Jacob, Matthew Spangler, Leean Kim Torske, Lindsey Grant, Emily Pérez, Sasha West, Jill Meyers, Mónica Ibarra Parle, Hillary Shedd, Claire Boyles, Abe Streep, Kathy Kline, Terry Benson, Leslie Shipman, Lindsay O'Donovan, and Miwa Messer.

Jennine Crucet Palacio, for making the second person change for me. And Claire Messud, for making the first person do the same.

To Warren Wilson, especially Deb Allbery, and to Rita Banerjee, Christine Kitano, and Yanyi, whose lecture "A Formal Feeling" transformed this book.

My Wyoming friends: Arielle Zibrak, Tara and Josh Clapp, Morgan DeFoort, Maggie Bourque and Rick Fisher, Fawn and Evan Johnson, Julianna Mather, Kaijsa Calkins, Rachel Potter, Courtney Carlson, Teal Wyckoff, and Paul Covey.

Julia Obert—that first text you sent me saved me. Thank you for reading, editing, and being such exceptional support.

Acknowledgments

So much love to Karen Eustis, whose friendship and care are unmatched.

The Crescent Avenue girls: Dawn Fay and Amber, Stacy and Barbara, and Susanna.

To my Johnson family: Nate and Aimée Boutin-Johnson, Nick Johnson, Susan Y. Johnson, Allen Johnson and Susan Brody, Don and Susan A. Johnson, and all Johnson/Youngbergs.

To my parents, Nirmala and Patrick McConigley, my home.

And to the Martins, Paul, Finn, and Aoife: You always carry you.

And Lila, for always making ickinspick very leebossa.

For so many cold prairie walks: Lincoln.

To the hearts outside my body: Juniper Nirmala and Marigold Laxmi.

And every thanks to Michael, always, for Michael. This book would not exist if not for the mini-tinis, hotel stays, meals, pep talks, and all the times you watched the girls so I could work. MOTL and every yotta is for you. I love you beyond measure. I love you beyond words.

Nina McConigley is the author of the story collection *Cowboys and East Indians*, which was the winner of the PEN Open Book Award and the High Plains Book Award. She has received grants and fellowships from the National Endowment for the Arts, the Radcliffe Institute, Bread Loaf Writers' Conference, Vermont Studio Center, and the Sewanee Writers' Conference. She was a recipient of the Wyoming Arts Council's Frank Nelson Doubleday Memorial Writing Award and a finalist for a National Magazine Award for her columns in *High Country News*. Her work has also appeared in *The New York Times*; *Orion*; *O, The Oprah Magazine*; *Virginia Quarterly Review*; and Salon, among other outlets. Born in Singapore and raised in Wyoming, she now lives in Colorado.

A NOTE ON THE TYPE

This book was set in Janson, a typeface long thought to have been made by the Dutchman Anton Janson, who was a practicing typefounder in Leipzig during the years 1668–1687. However, it has been conclusively demonstrated that these types are actually the work of Nicholas Kis (1650–1702), a Hungarian, who most probably learned his trade from the master Dutch typefounder Dirk Voskens. The type is an excellent example of the influential and sturdy Dutch types that prevailed in England up to the time William Caslon (1692–1766) developed his own incomparable designs from them.

Composed by North Market Street Graphics,
Lancaster, Pennsylvania

Designed by Casey Hampton